D0617002

Advance Praise for

Forsooth

"*Forsooth* is a heartwarming reminder that we are all the star of our own show—worthy of not just the spotlight, but love. You'll be rooting for Calvin from start to finish."

—Jason June, *New York Times* bestselling author of *Out of the Blue*

"*Forsooth* is proof that nobody overcomes disaster like theater kids! Whether it's a play going haywire or navigating coming out to his religious family, Calvin survives it all with a big heart and bigger laughs. A must-read for the shining stars in your life!"

—Adam Sass, award-winning author of *The 99 Boyfriends of Micah Summers* and *Surrender Your Sons*

"*Forsooth* dives into the confusing collision of faith, friendships, and first crushes with a winning combination of tenderness and laugh-out-loud humor. I fell hard for Calvin Conroy, in all his messy glory, from the very first page. This is a book I wish I could deliver via time machine to my thirteen-year-old self."

—Chad Lucas, author of *Thanks a Lot, Universe*

"This book is unputdownable! A propulsive, witty, heart-filling read, *Forsooth* is a story I wish I'd had when I was a kid. It is at once a primer on friendship, an exploration of crushes and love, and a peek into the brain—and heart—of delightful, relatable Calvin. Even as we watch him crash and burn (sometimes literally!), we're rooting for Calvin and his friends every step of the way. A fresh, needed story of theater kids navigating the world on social media and IRL."

—Emily Barth Isler, author of *AfterMath*

Forsooth

Jimmy Matejek-Morris

CAROLRHODA BOOKS
MINNEAPOLIS

Carolrhoda Books®
An imprint of Lerner Publishing Group, Inc.
241 First Avenue North
Minneapolis, MN 55401 USA

For reading levels and more information, look up this title at www.lernerbooks.com.

Cover illustration by Marina Pérez Luque.
Image credits: bubaone/DigitalVision Vectors/Getty Images.

Main body text set in Bembo Std.
Typeface provided by Monotype Typography.

Library of Congress Cataloging-in-Publication Data

Names: Matejek-Morris, Jimmy, 1985– author.
Title: Forsooth / Jimmy Matejek-Morris.
Description: Minneapolis, MN : Carolrhoda Books, [2023] | Audience: Ages 11–14. | Audience: Grades 7–9. | Summary: "When thirteen-year-old theater kid Calvin sets out to make a movie with his friends, drama ensues, forcing him to sort through his first crushes, face family tensions, and learn how to be true to himself" —Provided by publisher.
Identifiers: LCCN 2022040845 (print) | LCCN 2022040846 (ebook) | ISBN 9781728457598 | ISBN 9781728493886 (ebook)
Subjects: CYAC: Interpersonal relations—Fiction. | Gay people—Fiction. | Friendship—Fiction. | Middle schools—Fiction. | Schools—Fiction.
Classification: LCC PZ7.1.M37644 Fo 2023 (print) | LCC PZ7.1.M37644 (ebook) | DDC [Fic]—dc23

LC record available at https://lccn.loc.gov/2022040845
LC ebook record available at https://lccn.loc.gov/2022040846

Manufactured in the United States of America
1-50787-50126-5/1/2023

For my sister, Megan, who never did theater
but has always been a star in my eyes

PROLOGUE

Okay, so you're standing on the stage, right? Surrounded by these cardboard cobblestone houses. Everyone's staring at you, but it's not because you're the dreamy prince with the loose black curls and gap-toothed grin that makes all the seventh-grade drama maidens swoon. That's Jonah. It's because you're holding this glass shoe in your hands, you know the one, and I guess that's why you're called the Footman. Except instead of a glass heel it's this silver slipper that Maia's mother spent hours hotgluing sequins all over. They glisten in the spotlight.

"Surely," Jonah says with a dramatic flip of the head, "there must be another eligible foot from whence this shoe came."

"Forsooth," you whisper. That's not the project-for-the-folks-in-the-back voice that Miss H. insisted you use because she could only afford to rent microphones for the leads. You scan the sea of heads. Your parents are out there somewhere, and your snooty sister, Sarah, and probably a few talent scouts if they've heard anything about Jonah's swoopy hair or Kennedy's gorgeous voice.

Speaking of your best friend, Kennedy glides onto the stage. There's a collective swoon as if the audience somehow didn't expect she'd be back for the final scene. Even without the sparkling purple ball gown, she's stunning. A strategic reddish-brown curl dangles along the side of her freckled face, perfectly hiding the rental microphone taped to her cheek. You can tell she's a good actress because you'd never know this timid peasant has over 5,000 Instagram followers. "If you please, sir," she softly implores. God bless technology reserved for the leads. Even though her whispered voice trembles, everyone can hear.

"FORSOOTH!" you shout as you realize people in the back row might have missed the pivotal line that called her onto the stage. Kennedy jumps. Whoops, too loud. Somebody in the audience snickers and you can bet it's Sarah. Sisters.

You sneer into the crowd, but all you can see are faceless heads. Hundreds of heads. Hundreds of heads times two equals thousands of eyes. And they are all looking at you. You gulp. Do the lights feel hotter than they did during dress rehearsal? A string of sweat drips down your forehead, answering your question. You wipe it away with the hand that's still gripping the silver slipper. The shoe *thunk*s against your head.

What does "forsooth" even mean, and why can't you remember what comes next, and couldn't they have sprung for an extra microphone, and seriously, why are these lights like a million flipping degrees?

Your hand is soggy. Maia scowls at you from one side, her eyes sending death rays. Who knows whether this is because she's playing the wicked step-mother and she's supposed to look mad or because the heat of this spotlight is melting the glue that her mother worked so hard on and there are glittery sequins sticking to your soaked palms?

Little black spots dance before your eyes, and the room starts spinning. You take two steps back and find yourself stumbling into Jonah. He catches you, his warm brown arm reaching around from behind and squeezing your chest. You can feel his heart thumping against your back. Your second-best friend has got you. Literally.

"You can do this," he whispers. And curse you,

technology-set-aside-for-leads, his private encouragement is blasted throughout the auditorium.

It almost doesn't matter. For one brief second, you feel safe in his arms.

Until he pushes you upright, and the dark spots return. You force out whatever words you think make sense: "I have foundeth another lady." You take a few shaky steps toward Kennedy. She smiles, but you can tell it's only a lips smile. Her Wicked-green eyes are terrified. (*Wicked* the musical, obviously, but is that a hint of anger mixed in too?) You're ruining everything, you fool. But you can save this. And you have to. For Kennedy.

Like a pro, she lifts the hem of her patchwork dress, kicks off her slipper, and extends her leg in your direction. She's doing everything for you. Put the slipper on her foot. But you can't stop talking: "And looketh," you exclaim, using your back-of-the-room voice. "She has the same feet as that cleaner woman you danced with at the ball. Face looks familiar too."

"Just put the shoe on her, Calvin!" the prince commands.

"Forsooth, your majesty," you say, stepping away from Jonah. You spin toward Kennedy, but the room is spinning even quicker.

Why won't everyone stop laughing?

Maia storms forward, arms out, trying to steal the shoe, no doubt.

You squeal.

That's when you notice the blinking red light, way in the back of the room, because of course this is the night they decided to film the show. You swear you can make out the smug grin of the camera person, and that's the last thing you see as it all becomes too much with the lights and the laughter and the sweat and the sequins that are stuck to your fingers.

"It fits," you exclaim as the room fades to black, and you fall off the stage.

Seventy-three days later,
but who's counting?

CHAPTER 1

"Promise me," Kennedy says as she snaps the cap back onto her purple gel pen, "that you won't read this until you get home." She blows on the signature and swishes her pale hand back and forth over the text in an attempt to dry my final *have a nice summer* before we actually go out and do so. She gently closes the flimsy paperback yearbook and hands it to me.

"Okay." I shrug.

"You gushing your heart out to him or something?" Jonah teases Kennedy. His curly hair swishes as he shoots her a questioning glance.

I laugh, because everyone knows that Kennedy and Jonah belong together. Or at least, everyone *would* know that if they actually cared about my friends and me, but drama kid drama is not high on the list of things our seventh-grade classmates care about. Unless, of course, you fall off the stage. Then it's all anybody can talk about for the past seventy-three days.

It wasn't so bad at first—everyone in the audience rising to their feet and shouting "Call 911!" because suddenly, I was the star. *And Miss H. didn't think I could play a lead.* A pair of hands yanked my shoulder, and I opened my eyes with a gasp. The room erupted into applause. My first standing ovation.

The ambulance came next.

I texted Kennedy as Mom and Dad whispered buzzwords with the doctors: Nothing broken. Ice packs. Therapy.

Don't sweat it, Kennedy's message said. People make careers of falling off the stage all the time. Ever hear of The Play that Goes Wrong?

Uh. I just starred in it, I replied.

After I was sent home with nothing but a bruised elbow and damaged pride, the whispered conversations began. Once everyone sees you aren't actually hurt, the "poor kid"s turn into "loser" and "Forsooth!" and—

BRRRRINGINGGGINGINGING. The school bell rings, and with that, the worst year of my life is over. We are officially eighth graders. The entire class erupts in celebration, popping out of our seats and shoving our way out of Miss Aarons's English classroom for the last time.

"What a year," Kennedy proclaims as we emerge into the bustling hallway. She's not talking to us, though. She holds her phone out in front of us to share the scene with her online fans, the Kennedians. Ever since she scored three national commercials and a cameo in the fifteenth episode of *Twister Sisters*, her followers have clamored for more, and whoa boy has she delivered.

"The bell sings, and the caged bird flaps her wings," she recites dramatically. "Yes. You see. The bird is free." She flips the camera to selfie mode. "And that bird. My friends? That bird is me." She chuckles. "Too cheesy? Sorry folks, but it's summer, and we are freeeeeee!" The camera pans the hallway one last time. She lifts her finger to stop recording right before it hits my face. She almost always stops right before showing me on her page because my parents insisted. I want to be famous like Kennedy, a star, but they want me to "protect my privacy" and "have a childhood," whatever that means. On the rare occasion when I do appear, Kennedy never tags me and refers to me as C. So far, my parents haven't noticed.

"You okay?" I ask Kennedy once I'm sure it's only the three of us again. We've stopped at my locker, and I start shoveling junk into my backpack.

"Of course," she says, but I've never seen a more wooden performance from Longfellow Middle School's leading lady. "I'm just remembering." She glances toward the drinking fountain. I wonder what memory she's picturing. Maybe the time Miss H. posted the cast list for *The Sound of Music* above that very drinking fountain. It was the first year we were old enough to try out, and Kennedy and I approached the list hand in hand.

"OMG! Liesl," she cried when she spotted her name.

I scanned the list three times before finding mine, all the way at the bottom: *Calvin Conroy: Monk Understudy.*

My heart plummeted. "I don't remember a monk in the movie."

Kennedy squeezed my hand a little tighter. "This is perfect," she said with a sparkle in her voice. "You'll have time to help *me* practice, and you and I will know what a huge mistake she made.

Our little secret. My true Rolf." She bumped her shoulder into mine.

Something about the way she said it made me believe it was true. Kennedy always made me believe I *could*, even though the rest of the world knew I couldn't. When we met Jonah (aka Friedrich von Trapp) that year in the show, he was equally great. We became a best friend trio, inseparable. Well, until I ruined Jonah's big scene this year, and he got kind of weird, always keeping a Kennedy-sized space between us.

I study my two best friends while we're at our lockers. Kennedy checking her Likes. Jonah, noticing me noticing her and playfully rolling his eyes. It feels almost normal. Almost right. I like to think of my friends as the night sky. Kennedy: the brightest star in the galaxy. Jonah: the shy planet that will surprise you with its twinkle when it comes out from hiding. And me: the plane that almost tricks you for a second.

I grin as I close my locker door for the last time and slip my bag back onto my shoulders.

Kennedy nods toward the yearbook that I'm still hugging to my chest. Softly, she says, "Just call me when you've read it, okay?"

"Intrigue!" Jonah exclaims.

My face reddens so I almost match the lockers that line the hall. Did she profess her love for me? That would ruin everything! I'm not her leading man—the prince to her Cinderella, the Seymour to her Audrey, the Birdie to her Bye Bye. That's been Jonah in every three-person musical we've performed in his basement since we met.

Jonah yanks the book from me and flips through the black-and-white faces of my classmates, his eyes scanning for Kennedy's purple pen.

Kennedy swats at the book, crinkling the pages. "I'm warning you."

"Stop it," I command both of them, but nobody listens to the background artist when the leads are fighting. I lunge for the book. Jonah ducks away from me, nearly tripping over his backpack, which is resting on the floor beside his still-open locker. Inspired, I hop onto his back, grasping for the floppy glossy cover from behind.

"Get off," he says with a laugh, spinning me around.

I clench his chest to avoid falling to my doom. My hips bounce against his back and my legs flail.

"WATCH IT, CALVIN CONROY," Maia

shrieks, coming out of a nearby classroom, sounding as nasty as she did during her Wicked Stepmother performance.

"Not my fault, Maia Ruiz," I half apologize, half spit.

Jonah tilts sideways and I nearly roll on top of her. I clutch Jonah's chest more tightly as Maia swats at my foot. Her eyes lock with mine for a moment. Flecks of golden honey seem to flare in her brown irises as she pushes past us and heads for the buses waiting outside.

I can't hold on much longer and begin to slide off my friend's back. I reach out in one last desperate attempt and finally grasp the yearbook.

"Let! Go!" I call as I thunk to the floor, but he doesn't. There's a horrible *riiiiiippp* as exactly one half of the yearbook joins me on the floor. Jonah nearly stumbles on top of me, twisting at the last second and instead smacking against the lockers with a horrible clank. He rubs the back of his head with the hand that isn't holding the other half of my yearbook.

"Are you fuh-reaking kidding me?" I mutter, glad my mom isn't at school to hear me almost curse. I push myself to my feet. Mom's gonna be so ticked, and my friends both know it. She only gave me the money to buy this thing so she could show it off to her family and church friends. What is she supposed to show them now?

"Calvin . . ." Jonah begins to apologize. He holds out the handful of loose pages.

"Just give it to me," I sigh as I snatch the sheets from him.

"I didn't want things to end like this," Kennedy says with a frown.

"A little late for that," I grunt, trying to sound tough while struggling to hide a smile. That's the closest Jonah and I have been since the Incident, and wrestling in the hallway was actually kind of fun. Is this how the obnoxious loud kids feel all the time? In spite of the damaged yearbook, I feel my spirits lifting. This summer is going to be a fresh start for the three of us. You know the end of *Grease* where they dance down the halls linking arms singing yabba bad banana yip skippety dip ding dong? That's us. We are going to be fine, and it all starts now.

With a grand spin that'd look even more amazing if they could see the dramatic flutter of the cape I'm imagining, I walk away, calling over my shoulder, "But there's always eighth grade."

For a supporting actor who ruined an entire play, I can certainly make a star exit.

I peek over my shoulder to see if they've even noticed, but their eyes . . .

Their lips . . .

They're kissing.

CHAPTER 2

"Wait, wait, wait, wait, wait!" I smack the door as the bus pulls away. It lurches to a reluctant stop. Mr. Murphy opens the door and rolls his eyes as I clamber up the stairs. "Thank you, sir," I say in between gasps for air. I can't imagine what Mom would say if she had to come get me on the last day of school because I'd missed the bus because I was watching my best friends make out after destroying the yearbook she bought for me.

I've always known Jonah and Kennedy would get together eventually. I've always *wanted* it to happen. So why did seeing it make me feel so . . . confused?

Heads peek at me from every single seat, and the blood rushes to my brain. It's like I'm on the stage all over again. I tighten my shoulders and squeeze the yearbook fragments in my fist. *Don't cry.*

I refuse to make eye contact with anyone as I make my way down the aisle, instead staring at the long black ridges that run along the gritty floor.

After this bus ride, there'll be a full summer for everyone to forget about the Incident of the Spring Musical. A full summer for Jonah to forgive me for ruining his show. A full summer for me to watch my best friends' love story grow because it is beautiful and sweet and not at all surprising and I am perfectly fine with it.

And if Mom has anything to say about it, a full summer of me finding Jesus. I didn't even realize He was lost until she signed me up for summer youth choir at church. "It'll be fun," she claimed. "Plus, maybe it'll help with the . . ." Her voice faded as she stretched out her hand and wobbled it around, too embarrassed to describe what I'd actually done out loud in case Jesus had somehow missed the show. "You know."

I don't have time to worry about that now, though. If I don't choose a seat soon, I'll find myself in Bullywood, aka the back of the bus, so I quickly tuck into the first empty row I can fi—

Dang it. Slouched down and pressed against the window, invisible from the aisle, is my next-door neighbor, Blake. He moved in six months ago, and we've spoken to each other approximately three times since then even though he's in two of my classes and we share a bus stop. He's quiet, but not the same kind of quiet as me. I'm quiet because my friends are so loud and don't give me a chance to speak. He's quiet because he doesn't have any friends.

"Sup?" he says, barely looking up from his phone as I lower myself onto the bumpy brown seat beside him.

"Nothing." I secretly try to channel Kennedy, who can burrow into someone's head through observation and pull out the truth hidden inside. Character studies, she calls them, but I know what they really are: X-rays into the heart. I imagine the hum of an X-ray machine as I attempt to figure out my next-door neighbor.

Blake wears tight pants and a tighter black T-shirt emblazoned with the name of some band I don't recognize. I can't tell whether this is a look or if he's outgrown his clothing. His right arm is covered in pen-drawn doodles like he's some kind of tattooed rebel, perfectly matching his strategically spiked hair. Stubble decorates his chin. I haven't even started shaving yet. I'm almost jealous. My hand absently strokes my cheek, wondering what it would feel like if it were coated with tiny, chopped hairs.

Blake's eyes shift to me, puzzled. "Suuuup?" he says again, but this time with a *stop being a creeper* tone.

"I, uh . . ." I freeze because what would a normal person even say here? "You're in AV Club, right?" I ask.

"Yeah," he replies. "You noticed?"

I gesture toward the phone as if every other kid on this bus doesn't have their nose glued to a screen, as if Blake is somehow special. "Your club filmed my show."

"We did," he admits. "I noticed you too." His lips curl into a smile.

My eyes widen. So he was the smirk that filmed the school show the night I fell off the stage. Of course. I wonder how many times he's watched my worst moment.

He must be doing a character study of his own, as he quickly changes the subject, pointing instead toward the yearbook pages in my hands. "What the heck happened here?" he says, except he doesn't say *heck*.

"Kennedy and Jonah," I say, as if that explains everything.

"Dang," he says, using a stronger word.

I wince on behalf of my mother, who can't even handle when I'm curse-adjacent. My eyes turn down to the torn pages. I'm close enough to home, so let's see what this secret message is all about. I flip to the autograph section. Kennedy's purple penmanship pops off the page. There's a hint of silver glitter shimmering in the ink. *My dearest Calvin, I'm going to miss you so much next year . . .*

"WHAT?" I cry out.

Blake nearly drops his phone. "What the heck, man?" is the PG version of what he snaps.

"Will you stop with the cursing?" I bite back.

"Sorry." He slouches farther down in the seat and returns his attention to the phone, flicking his fingers across the screen even though I can clearly see it's off. I frown. My best friend may be leaving, but at least I *have* a friend. Poor guy.

"Kennedy's moving," I offer.

"That sucks," he says, as if he understands any of this. "Stinks," he corrects himself. "Smells real ickalicious."

I can't help but laugh at that one before returning to the message to fill in the pieces. Blake leans in to read over my shoulder.

My dearest Calvin, I am going to miss you so much next year. My heart cries to think of a year without you by my side, but I've hit the big time. The New York Youth Academy for the Performing Arts! I am one step closer to the dream, but I will never forget my first and favorite fan. XOXO Kennedy

"Fan?" Blake reads aloud.

"The biggest," I agree. I didn't even know she applied to NYYAPA. And now she's going! Why didn't she tell me in person? She writes it in a freaking yearbook note? This doesn't make any sense. Kennedy is supposed to love drama. Me bawling my eyes out, clinging to her as I beg her not to go. Jonah a messy heap on the floor, wondering what he'll do without his beloved. Does he even know the secret hiding behind those lips he was kissing? Was it a goodbye kiss? "What the heck, Kennedy?!"

I realize I may have said this last bit using my project-for-the-folks-in-the-back voice. There's a laugh and a not-so-quiet "Loser" from Bullywood. Everyone is staring at me.

"I am not a loser!" I shout back. My words bounce down the aisle. So does the laughter that follows, the echo filling the bus.

"Everyone close your windows. Don't want him falling out the bus."

More laughing. "Or maybe we do."

"Ryyyyyyyannn," the bus driver warns the bully, glancing into the rearview mirror, but it's too late to stop the words from stinging.

Black spots overwhelm my vision. It feels like I'm back on that auditorium floor again, gasping for air.

As the bus takes a sharp turn, I find myself sliding sideways into my seatmate. My head falls onto a shoulder that smells like too much deodorant.

I cringe myself upright. "I am so. So. Sorry." This day could not get any worse. "It's just . . . sometimes my head gets a little, uh, loud and I start to get dizzy, and now Kennedy's moving, and she's the only one who even tried to understand and told me at least I could still be a slapstick star, which is like, not the worst idea, and totally no offense to Jonah, but when I ruined his big scene, things got weird, and now they're in love, and she's leaving, and it'll be him and me all day every day, and oh my gosh who's going to star in the school shows, and what the heck am I supposed to tell my mom about *this*?" I wave the yearbook in Blake's face.

I'm so embarrassed and overwhelmed and can totally feel tears coming on and know the taunts will spread even further if anyone sees.

Blake says, "Breathe, Calvin. Breathe," with a kindness I would not expect from a guy with no friends and spiky hair. "It's going to be okay."

He's still a blob-ish blur in my vision, but I almost believe him. "They stop watching?" I whisper.

"Don't worry about them," he says, as if it's that easy. "Look at me and breathe." He takes a deep breath, in and out. In and out. He gestures for me to follow his lead, and slowly, the world returns, starting with Blake's storm-cloud-colored eyes, followed by his slightly crooked nose, and finally his fully crooked smile.

Still guiding my breaths, Blake gives me a subtle nod. His gaze never breaks from mine.

I suddenly realize he is holding my hand. He doesn't let go until we've reached our stop.

KENNEDY

Did you read it yet, Calvin?
Are you okay?
Cal?

Sent.

CHAPTER 3

Friends hold hands all the time, I tell myself as I stumble over my own feet through the front door of my house. There's a huge clatter. So much for sneaking in to avoid Mom and Sarah. At least Dad's still at work.

"Is that my eighth grader?" Mom sings from the kitchen in her chipper *We have company so you'd better behave* voice. I forgot that Tuesday afternoon means Mom's Bible Study, which is like a book club for church nerds who like to gossip. "I need a picture!" she coos above the murmur of her friends' voices. I scan the walls, which are covered in memorable moments featuring Sarah and me. *Need* is a strong word.

"Give me a second," I call back.

I dip down the hall toward my bedroom, thinking of all the times that Jonah and Kennedy have held my hand. Like when we read the cast lists each year or when we take our bows during curtain calls. See? All the time. Blake and I are friends now. That's all there is to it.

Right before I turn into my room, I glance up at the one hanging picture that isn't a photo of Sarah or me: a stoic painting of Jesus right outside my door, overlooking the hall but never truly seeing me. The bearded man's eyes are turned up as He contemplates the beam of light illuminating Him from above. It almost feels like He's avoiding me. Friends even hold friends' hands when praying at church. He can't argue with that.

Reassured, I duck into my bedroom and close the door behind me. I'm greeted by the sports posters my dad wishes I cared about. The baseball performers throw balls and swing sticks beneath the *Phantom of the Opera* masks I've taped to each of them. I toss my backpack onto the camo comforter that is as Me as the posters and pull out my phone. I've got a million messages from Kennedy.

So now she wants to talk.

Jonah has not said anything.

My thumbs dance around on the keys, unsure what to say. Why did you hide this from me? How dare you? You can't leave me. I type and delete each thought. I hope she can see the bouncing dots on her screen. Are you and Jonah dating now? Delete delete delete. I want to hold your hand. I laugh and wonder what she'd have to say about that.

A hurried knock *tap-tap-tap*s on my closed bedroom window. I scream and accidentally hit send on this last message. My phone drops onto my bed, and I whip my head around to see Blake standing in the shrubs outside the window.

I'm worried he's here to talk about hand-holding while Mom and her big-eared, loose-lipped friends are so close by. Bible Study is all cheese and crackers until you do something the ladies find questionable—then their tales spread through the community faster than the Good Word. Mom's strict rules strive to keep Sarah and me off her friends' radars, but there's only so much a parent's protection can do when you fall off the stage in front of the entire town. My reputation is not the only one that took a hit that night.

"Open up." Blake's voice is muffled through the glass.

After glancing over my shoulder, I tiptoe over and lift the window. "Uh, hi. What are you doing here?"

"So, listen," he begins.

"Here you are!" Mom exclaims, barging into my room. I whip around to face her. She's round, warm, and coated in floral-scented perfume. Her shoulder-length, dirty-blond hair is streaked with strands of gray.

Before I can reply, there's a brilliant flash as the phone in her hands captures my "so busted" eyes. I can't do anything without permission—hang out with friends, stay out past seven, listen to the explicit songs on my cast recordings—and permission is usually denied. I suspect window visitors would also be on the list of no-no's. She needs to leave before she spots Blake.

"Moooom," I groan, while realizing that fighting is futile. I flash my fakest toothy grin, place my hands on my hips and try to puff up as much as possible to block her view of the window behind me.

She snaps one photo. Then another. And another. She lowers the camera to study the first fifteen pictures. "Wait a second," she finally says. It takes every ounce of bravery inside me to not turn around and see if Blake is still out there. Her gaze flicks from the screen to my eyes to the screen. She zooms in on a picture with a swipe of her fingers.

Oh no. She must have spotted Blake hiding in the background. "What's this? What's going on?"

Where should I even begin? Maybe with a prayer.

Mom flips the screen around in my direction. The image is zoomed in on my puffy, panicked eyes. Oh. That. I take a deep breath, refusing to let myself cry. "Kennedy's moving."

"Aww, honey," she says, pity dripping from her voice. She steps forward, but I need to stop her from getting any closer to this window, so I run forward, arms out. Her large arms pull me in for a suffocating hug that I hope Blake can't see. Long stray hairs tickle my face. "Jesus and I will be your friends," she says, somehow forgetting that I still have another friend, Jonah, despite the fact that his upcoming bar mitzvah and our three-person plays are basically all that I ever talk about.

"Don't baby him, Mom." Sarah enters my room while chowing down on one of Mom's Bible Study cookies. Her blond hair is tied up in a loose *I-don't-care* braid that probably took her at least thirty minutes to not care about. She wears a baggy flannel shirt that's too warm for June in Massachusetts. I bet it belongs to Anthony, my sister's secret boyfriend that my "no boyfriends until you're eighteen" parents can never know about.

"I'm not babying him," Mom protests, without releasing me from her sweaty embrace.

She is, but I'm used to it by now.

I finally wiggle free from Mom's arms. "I'm fine. I promise. Now can you please leave me alone?" I know I'm being Sarah-level rude, but I've got to get Mom out of here before she becomes Dad-level mad. "I need a second."

"Only a second. Then it's Cheer-Up Cookie Time. And my friends want to say hi to you."

"Okay," I promise.

Mom turns to leave. A confetti cannon explodes in my stomach. She didn't see Blake. I'm safe.

"Hey," Sarah says as Mom reaches the doorway, "why is there a kid crouched outside your window?"

Mom whips around. I hurl a furious fireball at Sarah in my mind as my mother nearly knocks me over on her way to the window.

"Who are you?" she demands. Mom towers over Blake as he stands upright. My mother doesn't trust friends she hasn't carefully vetted. It took her years to warm up to Jonah and Kennedy, and sometimes she's still on the fence about them.

Blake shrinks farther into the shrubbery. "Blake Richardson, ma'am. I live next door." He holds up a pristine yearbook. "Calvin left his yearbook on the bus, and I, uh, wanted to be sure he got it back." He extends his arm, revealing a sweet pen drawing of an ostrich scribbled on his wrist.

Our eyes meet, and I feel this strange heart-thumping connection with my new friend.

Mom slides up the window screen and snatches the book from Blake's hand. She flips through to find my picture.

"Wait," I whisper to Blake. "Is this yours?"

"It's fine," he says. "I don't need it. Nobody signed it anyway."

Here he is saving my butt for the second time in an hour, and I couldn't even be bothered to sign his yearbook.

"Look at this face!" Mom announces to the room when she's arrived at my picture.

Blake smirks. "Well, I'll see ya round." He turns away.

I call, "Hey, wait!"

He pauses, turns back, and looks at me. I'm sure Mom and Sarah are watching too.

"You wanna grab some ice cream sometime?"

I haven't asked permission, so I prepare for Mom to protest. Without looking at her, I promise, "Don't worry. Jesus'll be there too."

Blake says, "Yeah. Totally. Though I'm not sure I understand the whole Jesus thing?"

Me neither, I want to reply, but instead I say, "I'll text you."

"Do you want my number?" he asks.

"Uh, yeah. Hold on a sec."

I scoot around my mother and scoop up my phone.

"Calvin . . ." my mom finally says with the polite kind of warning you get when you're being rude in front of company.

"Is everything okay in here?" one of Mom's friends inquires from the hallway. It seems my mother has spent enough time away from the group that their scandal senses have begun to tingle. Maia's mother, Mrs. Ruiz, pokes her head into the doorway. I can't help but wonder if anyone was home to greet Maia on her last day of school.

"Fine," my mother says, and without a second glance she escorts Maia's mother back toward the kitchen.

I return to the window, phone in hand. An unread

message from Kennedy shows an emoji handshake, and I realize that even if a fresh yearbook solves one problem, I've still got a million more.

"Okay if Jonah and Kennedy come too?" I ask Blake, guilt settling into my stomach because for once, I almost forgot my real friends, and I almost didn't mind.

CHAPTER 4

"Enjoy your double date," Sarah says as Blake and I pile out of the back seat of her car.

"It's not a double date. We're meeting Jonah and Kennedy."

"Exactly," she teases.

"Leave 'em alone, hon," her secret boyfriend, Anthony, says from the front seat. "Have fun, kids." He sounds like a grown-up trying too hard to be cool even though they're both only seventeen. His grin screams *Please Like Me* while his Patriots hat, church clothes, and goopy eyes for my sister say *Nope*.

I slam the door, and Sarah and Anthony pull away, off to a date of their own. Not that *this* is a date.

I look at Blake, embarrassed. "Sisters."

He shrugs. "I'm an only child."

We stride across the parking lot and into Cone-y Island: the Flavor Playground of Massachusetts. It's a pastel paradise that smells like freezer burn, chocolate sauce, and strawberries.

Jonah and Kennedy are waiting in a booth, both facing the door. There's a painful distance between them. They each smile as they notice me, but when they spot Blake by my side, their expressions diverge. As Jonah scrunches his brow and tilts his head, Kennedy's grin stretches wider. She races up to us and loops her hand around Blake's arm. "You brought me a goodbye present," she coos. "And a cutie, even."

Kennedy leads Blake to our booth and takes the place across from Jonah, pulling Blake in by her side.

"Sup, man," Blake says to Jonah.

"Hey," Jonah replies as I slide in beside him.

"So, I guess he's your date this evening," Blake says to me.

"What?" I blush. Jonah looks like he may throw up.

"Like your sister was saying," he tries to explain. "When she was joking. It's"—he gulps before looking to me nervously— "a joke?"

"We tend not to listen to Sarah," Jonah says dismissively.

"Besides"—I'm quick to change the subject, terrified that one of the hundred-something parishioners of St. Joseph's is within earshot—"Jonah and Kennedy are . . ."

I trail off, waiting for one of them to reveal the kiss. Jonah clears his throat, and Kennedy pulls out her phone to capture the awkward moment. "You mind?" she asks Blake after she's already taken a picture and shared it online.

"Uhhh . . ." Blake and I say at once. It kinda stings that Blake is now featured on her page more times than I am, and what is she even doing, trying to trick me into thinking that she's into someone besides Jonah?

Jonah hasn't wiped the scowl from his face. Why are they hiding their love from me?

I refocus. "A yearbook message, Kennedy? Really?"

Her smile fades away. "An autograph like that'll be worth a pretty penny one day," she says. I laugh because it's totally true, but it still hurts a little. "And I couldn't bear to see you brokenhearted," she adds.

My insides quiver. I reach across the table. She puts her hand in mine. Aha! A friend holding a friend's hand. And why shouldn't we? We've been best friends since second grade.

I remember the time she approached my family's table at this very ice cream parlor, and I had the nerve to be embarrassed about it. My eight-year-old self didn't want Sarah or my parents to know I was in the same class as the star from the Girl Scout Cookies commercial. Can you imagine how big a disappointment I'd be by comparison?

"I'm sorry, ma'am," I said to Kennedy, "but we don't need any Girl Scout Cookies at this time."

She looked at me for a moment, puzzled, then laughed and laughed and laughed. Legend has it, if you listen closely, you can still hear the echoes bouncing around the walls and rattling the freezers.

The sound was truly contagious. I was practically wheezing when I added, "Actually, maybe a box of Thin Mints."

"And an autograph?" she asked. She grabbed one of the kiddie crayons I wished I hadn't been using and scribbled her name across a napkin. I still have that napkin, which must be worth at least twice as much now.

That moment set the stage for our friendship. I can't believe I ever wanted to push her away.

"You can't leave," I say, panic creeping into my voice. I glance at Jonah, who stays silent. Guilt finally settles in, as I realize Jonah is losing his one true love—and here I brought some random guy, and she is ALL over him. Jonah may have ruined my yearbook, but I could be ruining his life. "How much time do we have?" I ask Kennedy.

"My dad says I can stay here with him through the summer, or head to New York early and live with my mom." Her mom has been in New York City since her parents got divorced, but I never in a million years thought Kennedy would want to join her after what happened. "NYYAPA has this summer acting program—"

"PLEASE STAY!" I blurt out, causing everyone to jump. I wait for Jonah to join me, but he still says nothing.

"I'll probably stick around here till the fall classes start," Kennedy admits as she releases my hand. "Now I gotta pee, and then we should order so that guy stops giving us the stink eye for hogging a booth."

I glance toward the counter and note the ice-cream-cold glare of the cashier. There's a reason this place isn't called Friendly's.

Once Kennedy has crawled over Blake and followed the neon arrow that points to the restrooms, I turn to Jonah and ask, "Are you okay?"

His finger traces the graffiti that covers the table. "I'm fine," he says in a voice that sounds the opposite.

"Then why aren't you fighting this? If anyone could convince her to stay, it's you."

"You don't know what you're talking about."

"Are you kidding me?" I argue. "She couldn't bear the thought of breaking your heart—"

"Calvin. My heart is fine." He says this with the tone of someone who has no heart at all. I almost expect to hear a creak as his rusty Tinman head rolls back. I follow his gaze and take in the ice-cream-cone-shaped lighting fixture that dangles above our table.

"It's okay if it's not. I'd understand. I'm here for you." I place my hand on Jonah's, because that is what friends do. Both Blake's and Jonah's eyes dart down toward our touching hands.

Jonah yanks his away and brings it to his lap. "What are you doing?"

"Uh, I thought that maybe you . . ." Somehow, it isn't quite as easy to say *friends hold hands all the time* out loud. I change the subject. "We should do some-thing. For Kennedy."

"Like a farewell gift?" Blake says. "Might be cool. I don't really know her that well or anything, but it's tough to move. If there's a way to make it easier for her—"

"What?" I cry out. "No. We need to convince her to stay."

Jonah finally looks at me, his eyes almost horri-fied. "Calvin. You need to let her go."

I want to scream: *Just admit you kissed her. Admit you love her.* But I can't, and he won't. I sometimes forget how private Jonah can be when he's not daz-zling us on the stage.

Blake looks from Jonah to me. "You know, I've always wanted to shoot a movie with real actors." I can't imagine how boring his AV Club projects must have been without actors. What was he film-ing before? Rocks?

Blake continues, "We could do little scenes rec-reating your favorite memories or something."

"That's not big enough," I say. "If we're going to change her mind, if we're going to convince her to stay, this has got to be huge. A full-length cin-ematic masterpiece. I'm talking big-budget values on no-budget wallets. I'm talking costumes, lights, cameras—"

"Action?" Jonah says with a laugh. He straightens slightly, finally almost interested. "It has been a while since we've done one of our little productions. Could I direct?"

"Sure." Blake shrugs.

"And I'll write a killer script!" I exclaim. "It'll be based on Kennedy's life, but fictionalized enough to work on another level, as an allegory." I hope I correctly used the term that Miss Aarons drilled into our heads in English class.

This is a brilliant idea. My mind begins flipping through all the memories that will inspire the scenes in our masterpiece. *So Moving That It Convinced Hometown Hero to Stay Here*, boasts the *Boston Globe* headline I'm picturing. "But it has to be a surprise. We'll unveil the finished product at the end of the summer, and then Kennedy will know exactly . . ." I trail off as Kennedy reappears at the head of the table.

"Exactly what?" she asks.

Blake, Jonah, and I freeze, a trio of deer in the headlights. "Uhhh," Jonah bumbles as Blake goes, "Welllll . . ."

Amateurs. I look up at Kennedy, pull my lips into a frown, and state, "I am so sorry, ma'am. But we don't need any Girl Scout Cookies at this time."

With a snort, she smacks my arm. "So, you're saying you need another autograph before I go?"

"Try a hundred."

We laugh, and I know it's going to be okay.

CHAPTER 5

I don't know who thought that having choir practice at 8 a.m. was a good idea, but here we are, Dad driving me to St. Joseph's on his way to work.

Jonah and Kennedy call Dad the General because he's *generally* not around, and when he is, he's always enforcing Mom's three Rs: Rules, Reputation, and Responsibility. Sarah and I are not his favorite people, but we try our best. Well, I do, anyway.

I fidget in the cool leather seat, taking in the new-car smell that makes no sense. Dad's had this truck for at least five years.

"So," Dad says, his gravelly voice slicing through the silence.

"So?" I ask. I look up at him wondering which of the three Rs I've violated this time. His features live up to the nickname—he's a solid man who likes to remind us that in his younger days, he was all muscle. Now, the seat belt strains against his soft belly.

"Your mom told me about the neighbor kid."

"Blake? Yeah, he's great. We're making this thing for Ken—"

"He should use the door." Dad doesn't smile.

"He was giving me my year—"

"Calvin, will you listen to me." His voice is sharp. It's not a question. I can almost hear Jonah and Kennedy saluting *Sir Yes Sir*, as they always do behind his back when Dad gets like this. "Your mother and I don't know how we feel about him." Dad keeps his eyes on the road. (R number one: Rules.) "We don't know him yet, and your mother has heard some things that concerned her."

I can't imagine what juicy tidbits the Bible Study group has heard about a new seventh grader when the other kids in the school couldn't even be bothered to talk to him, let alone sign his yearbook.

"Heard what?" I press.

"I don't know," Dad says.

"From who?"

"I don't know."

"Well, what do you *think*?"

He seems shocked, not used to having his own

opinions about my life. "I don't know," he says for a third time. "Isn't he kind of"—agonizing pause—"different?" (R number two: Reputation.)

My dad could not have seen Blake more than once or twice at the bus stop, so what gave him this impression? The spikey hair? The tight black clothes? The scribbled sleeves?

"I'm different too," I remind my father.

"No, you're not," Dad insists, taking his eyes off the road for a quick moment to glare at me.

"You don't become a star by being normal." I say this quietly because I can read the message hidden behind Dad's expression loud and clear. He doesn't believe in me.

"You become a star," Dad corrects as the car rolls to a stop, "by practicing."

"Next school show's not till fall."

"Then let's start with this." He gestures to the church. We're here.

I pop out of the car without so much as a goodbye.

"Calvin . . ." Dad says as I slam the door behind me. I turn back and salute the General before turning away to fulfill my R number three, Responsibility.

I plow through the lobby and thrust open the wooden double doors that lead into the church, nearly storming right into Maia. Of course, *she's* in summer youth choir.

She should be angry that I've almost crashed into her, but she looks relieved. "We're the youngest two here," she whispers.

At the front of the room, eleven or twelve high schoolers surround a brown upright piano. The glimmer of a cobweb connects old Ms. Clarkson from the bench to the keys. I wonder if she's moved from that seat since last Sunday.

"Okay, whatever," I grumble in response, still thinking about how my dad seemed physically pained by the mere suggestion of my pending superstardom.

"I was trying to be nice. What's your problem?" Maia demands, glaring at me.

"None of your business," I say as we walk down the aisle side by side. It should be big enough for both of us, but we keep bumping elbows. This feels like First Communion all over again.

"I thought we could be choir friends," she tells me with a particularly spirited bump.

I look her up and down. In the light streaming through the stained glass windows, her tan skin is red and purple and blue and green. Even her dark wavy ponytail has a magical glow.

"I'm not looking for friends right now."

"Well, maybe I am," Maia pushes back, and I suddenly remember who used to live next door to me before Blake. Nika, Maia's best friend, who moved to Texas last year. With Kennedy on her way out, maybe I have more in common with Maia than I thought.

I take on a kinder tone. "Honestly, this just isn't how I wanted to spend every Tuesday and Thursday this summer."

"And Sundays at ten," she adds.

Ugh. "Forgot about the performances," I groan.

"I believe they're called Mass," she says with a laugh.

"They are indeed, Miss Ruiz," a voice agrees from right behind us. I whip around to discover Father Paul, a tall ghostly man with hollow cheeks whose thinning mop of white hair looks multicolored in the window-filtered light. Maia and I scurry to join the rest of the choir, with the priest hovering close behind.

When he's reached the front, Father Paul leans against the piano, nearly knocking over Ms. Clarkson's sheet music in the process. She scoops it up with the slightest roll of the eyes.

"Gather round, kids," Father Paul commands,

even though we're clearly too old to be the children's choir. "On behalf of Ms. Clarkson and myself, welcome to what will surely be one of the most fulfilling summers of your young lives."

He's clearly trying to trick us into thinking that choir is an Art Form and not a fancy way of spelling *chore* with a miserable *i* stuck in the middle, but I know better.

"Now before I hand it over to Ms. C., I thought it'd be nice to hear what brought each of you here. Besides the car."

I snort, but nobody else even chuckles at the dad joke.

Father Paul winks at me before returning to the group: "Why did you all choose to spend your summer with us?"

Choose? Oh no.

We go around the room, and it's as bad as I feared.

Sarah's friend Rebecca: "Church music has always held a special place in my heart and soul."

Someone named Mary something-or-other: "Singing lifts my spirit and brings me closer to the Lord."

As the teens take turns stating something about their love of Jesus, I study the sculpted figure nailed to a cross behind the altar. A green fabric is draped over Jesus's outstretched arms. Skip me, skip me, skip me, I pray as Maia takes her turn, hitting all the points that would make my mom proud: praising God's love, serving the community, giving the gift of her voice to the Lord.

Father Paul places a hand over his heart when she finally stops. "Maia, that was wonderful."

She blushes, her cheeks reflecting a nice shade of stained-glass blue.

He turns to me.

Stained glass Jesuses (Jesi?) watch me from every window, so I have to choose my words carefully: "My name is Calvin Conroy, and I'm here because my parents think I'm not a star because I fell off the stage."

Two of the high schoolers chuckle, which, as it turns out, is even worse than random middle schoolers on the bus laughing at you.

Father Paul frowns as he says, "You're not here to be a star, Calvin. You're here for Him."

My face flushes.

"But with that said," he continues, "it is never too early to start thinking about our end-of-summer solo."

Maia's back straightens. She's probably been

thinking about that solo since before she signed herself up for this choir.

"Now we're not making any decisions yet, but I want every one of you"—I swear he's looking at me—"to have a chance. You will each prepare a song, and at the end of July, we'll hold auditions."

Auditions? My mind immediately races to the theater where it belongs, where *I* belong, and the idea of a choir solo almost doesn't sound so bad. Of course, I know it's a trick. No matter how well I nail "Food, Glorious Food" or "The Lonely Goatherd" in auditions, I'm 90 percent sure the actual performance will be some drab church song about bread or sheep. Still, Father Paul is seriously staring at me.

When he finally turns away, Maia leans in close and whispers, "Maybe we're not here to be stars, but if they want to give me that solo to prove once and for all that the school has been miscasting the female lead in our shows for years, I wouldn't argue."

I snort. Something about her tone sounds so familiar—and gives me an idea. Softly I ask, "Hey, how would you like the role of a lifetime?"

Maia smiles. "Oh? And what would that be?"

A hopeful grin spreads across my face. "Kennedy." Her smile vanishes, so I quickly add, "Kind of."

CHAPTER 6

Unlike its occupant, Kennedy's bedroom is quiet and understated. I sit with my feet on her bed, taking in the plain white walls and wobbly wooden furniture. Kennedy tells people she likes the blank slate so she can get into any character, but Jonah and I know her family has struggled with money for years. Things only got worse after her mom moved to New York. I still remember how much Kennedy resented her mother at the time.

"You really want to live with her now?" I ask as Kennedy rifles through her closet to decide what to pack and what to leave in the dust along with this room, this town, and me.

"It's NYYAPA," she replies over her shoulder.

"But your mom . . ."

"Mistakes were made," Kennedy says casually, as

if the empty auditorium seats meant nothing to her.

"How do you know you're not making another one?"

"Calvin. This could be my only shot. Prestigious art schools don't hand out scholarships every day."

"I know," I sigh, feeling selfish. Of course Kennedy deserves a chance to be a star. And okay, NYYAPA will get her there faster, but I don't buy that it's her *only* path to fame and glory. "But best friends don't come along every day either. Nothing's going to be the same without you."

Kennedy's shoulders droop. She closes the closet door and takes a seat on the bed beside me, reaching out her hand. I take it, because friends hold friends' hands all the time, though I wonder if that might get awkward once she and Jonah finally go public with their romance.

"Character study," Kennedy declares. Her green eyes scan me from the mess of hair on top to the bare feet on her comforter. "Thirteen-year-old boy. Best friend. Worried. Struggling. Big bumble in the past. Big change in the future." She pauses dramatically. I lean forward, glued to her every word as if she isn't describing me. "Big heart. Funny. Sweet. Needlessly needy. Capable of so much more than he realizes."

My insides tingle.

"Remember," she concludes, "the curtain cannot rise if it's never fallen."

Kennedy says her character studies help her understand a person and become a better actress, but when she directs her attention to Jonah and me, she helps us understand ourselves too. She makes me feel like everything is going to be almost okay.

I smile at her. Character studies are *her* specialty, but I think I see her too. Hopeful girl. Reaching for the stars. Trying to shine bright enough to banish the darkness that hovers over her family.

"You know you're already good enough," I say.

"I can be better."

"*Impossible*," I sing like Cinderella's fairy godmother.

Kennedy smiles, releases my hand, and rises to her feet again. "You only think that because you don't know how much more is out there waiting for me."

Did she just call me small-minded? I'm clearly not getting anywhere with her. I need help. "Where's Jonah?" I ask.

"He's not coming."

"Did . . . something . . . happen between you two?" I throw open the door for the kissversation.

She slams it in my face with a resounding "No."

Something definitely happened.

"Actually," she says, "I gotta get ready for a thing. You should head out now."

A thing? What thing? She's the one who invited me over. I want to protest, but I realize I'd better go too. It's clear that Kennedy's heart is set on NYY-APA unless we do something drastic. The movie is our only hope, and we aren't getting anywhere without a script.

When I get home, I wave to Mom and race to my room to start wordsmithing.

The screen on my laptop is as blank as my stare. What in the world could possibly convince Kennedy that she is already enough?

The city is calling her, but it's not like every famous person is from New York. I can think of at least two who are from Massachusetts! (That guy from the commercial and the featured soloist on that cast recording.) Maybe she needs a reminder that stars actually pop brighter against the night sky the farther you get from the big city lights.

My fingers begin to fly, and soon enough, I have our story.

27-year-old Melody Monarchy stands before the press in a beautiful ball gown, holding an armful of trophies: an Emmy, a Grammy, an Oscar, and a Tony. Cameras flash. The crowd swoons.

REPORTER
Melody Monarchy, Melody Monarchy, over here. How does it feel to be the first person to win all four awards of the coveted EGOT in a single night?

MELODY MONARCHY
These ole things? *(She laughs.)*
Truly magical.

REPORTER
Tell us where you got your start!
New York, probably?

MELODY MONARCHY
Oh, Heavens no.

Melody Monarchy freezes. The cast recording of "Memory" from Cats begins to play. Record scratch! The song is replaced with a

Hamilton-inspired "rewind." Melody Monarchy, the reporter, and the adoring crowd throw their arms in the air and dance backward. We flash back in time to her small-town beginnings, the friends that stood by her as she became a star, and the difficult choice she once faced to stay or leave it all behind.

One scene done, but it somehow already feels like more than enough. I throw a chef's kiss into the air and text Maia, Blake, and Jonah: It's showtime.

CHAPTER 7

Jonah and I wait in his basement for the rest of the crew to get here. The wooden ceiling is home to an elaborate maze of wires, pipes, and two flickering light bulbs that do their best to illuminate the cold concrete space. This is the first time we've been completely alone since the Incident, and the silence between us knows it.

My phone buzzes. A text from Kennedy. It's like she realizes we're missing a Kennedy-sized space. Wanna hang? Ice cream emoji. Dancing red dress emoji. Squirrel emoji.

How am I supposed to talk to her right now without spoiling the biggest surprise of the summer? I'll get back to her later. I tuck my phone back into my pocket.

"Can you help me with this stuff?" Jonah asks as

he hoists an overflowing cardboard box off the stage. Okay, so it's not actually a stage, just a place where the concrete floor is three inches higher than the surrounding floor, but it's been home to countless Basement Productions masterpieces starring Jonah, Kennedy, and (sometimes featuring) me. Right now, it's buried beneath boxes of Jonah's dad's old stuff. His dad died a few years ago, and until last year, the entire upstairs was a shrine to his memory. Then one day, Jonah's mom started dating again. The next thing we knew, our stage had become a storeroom, and Basement Productions was out of business.

I scoop a cardboard box up from the exact place where Kennedy Dreamed a Dream that her parents weren't getting a divorce. (They were, but the performance still gives me chills whenever I think about it.) "Have you talked to her?" I ask as I recall her genuine tears during that haunting song.

Jonah shakes his head and shrugs. "I see her posts." Why won't he say anything about the kiss?

Rather than contemplate that mess, I shift the banged-up box against my hip so I can free my right arm and snoop through the contents. Some button-down shirts, a handful of neckties, a wedding album, and a framed photo of Jonah and his family. Jonah can't be more than six in the picture, and his sister, Michal, must be about three. Their dad had copper skin like Michal, while Jonah and his mom have darker brown complexions. My parents occasionally use the word *Black* with a hushed tone as if it's on their list of forbidden words, so Jonah and I never really talk about that either.

I study his family's big grins in the photo. They all look so happy standing in front of the Golden Gate Bridge. I can't even imagine his loss. His hurt. "You must really miss your dad," I say at the exact moment that Jonah states, "There's something I have to tell you about Kenn . . . Hey! Get out of there," he commands, noticing my snooping.

He snatches the box from my arms.

"Sorry," I say, mostly bummed that I interrupted his Kennfession.

Clutching the cardboard box, he spins away and freezes with his back to me. "It's just . . ." He trails off, and I wait for him to say more. There's a sigh. "It's like . . ." He stops again. He slowly turns to face me. His eyes are brimming with tears. "With my bar mitzvah this summer, it's like, how am I supposed to do this without my dad?" He can't go on, but he doesn't have to.

I take the box back from him, set it on the floor, and pull my friend into a hug. He doesn't recoil like he did in the restaurant, instead wrapping his arms around me and squeezing. I can feel his tears streaming down my neck. His body heaves with every breath. He smells like the peppermint candies they give out in restaurants, with a hint of sweat.

"Am I interrupting something?" a voice asks from the stairs.

Jonah immediately releases me and whips around as Maia comes down the stairs. He brushes the tears away with a quick swipe of his hand, and he's such a pro that you wouldn't even know he'd been crying. "Maia?"

"No," I say, excited to reveal this surprise casting choice. "I'd like you to meet Kennedy! I mean, uh, Melody Monarchy."

"Slow your train, dude," she says. "I said I'd hear you out. I never said I'd do it. And don't ever call me Kennedy again. It's insulting that you think I have so little talent."

A grin spreads across Jonah's face. "She's definitely got the attitude for it," he tells me with a smile.

"And the voice of an angel," I chime in. "Totally going to win the church solo. I guarantee it."

"You what?" she asks.

"I . . . yeah," I say, floundering a bit. "I'll make sure you get the solo."

Maia crosses her arms. "How?"

With my bluff called, I have to think fast. "By . . . helping you practice."

"Uh, I'm a better singer than you."

Rude, but we need her. "So is Kennedy, but who did she go to as her official, unofficial voice coach for every single school audition?"

"Fine, I'll do it," Maia says with a laugh. "But why does it feel like I've made a deal with the devil?"

Before I can respond, Jonah's little sister's voice echoes into the basement: "It's Mee-hall." Michal clarifies her name to Blake as she leads him down the stairs. She's a small girl with a big voice who shares Jonah's gap-toothed grin, plus a few bonus missing teeth on either side. Her curly hair is pulled back into a puff that explodes behind her head. Blake, dressed all in black, contrasts starkly with her head-to-toe pink.

"And you're Maia, right?" Blake asks, shaking her hand like a gentleman.

"AKA Melody Monarchy." She rolls her eyes.

"But you said Iiiiii could be the lead," Michal whines to Jonah. It's a good thing Jonah's not in charge of casting. Michal is only nine, and she's not an artiste like Maia, Jonah, Blake, or even me.

"We'll find something else for you to do," Jonah promises, and I realize he must be on summer babysitting duty again while his mom works.

I try to keep us moving by suggesting, "Jonah, you should probably play Johnny Tomkins, the leading man."

He shakes his head. "I'm directing. That's it."

"But you always play the leads."

"Maybe I'm ready for something new," he says. There's a secret hidden behind his words that I can't extract. I wonder if this is what he was trying to tell me earlier.

I look to Blake, the obvious second choice. He can read my mind. "Can't film *and* act," he says as though he's never heard of a double threat or a tripod. "Why don't you play the part, Calvin?"

"Me? The male lead? Oh, I don't think so."

"Calvin, you can totally do it," Jonah interrupts, placing a hand on my shoulder. "You're a star."

The words and the feel of his hand send a jolt of electricity through me. "But who will play Melody's kindhearted, klutzy confidant, Kelvin Kenray?"

Maia chuckles. "I have a stuffed chicken that squawks when you squeeze it."

I frown, and her smile melts.

"Sorry." I can tell she means it. She clearly doesn't want to lose her edge with the church solo.

Michal steps forward and clears her throat. "Ahem."

Jonah nods at her. "Works for me. I like the gender-swapped casting. It's modern."

Is he serious? "Kid, I appreciate the confidence," I say to Michal, "but a role of this magnitude—"

"It doesn't have to be a big role," Blake interrupts. "You haven't even written the whole script yet, have you?" Clearly, he isn't part of this group yet if he doesn't realize how essential I am to Ken . . . I mean how essential Kelvin Kenray is to Melody Monarchy.

I wait for anyone else to speak up, but the room stays silent. Maia shrugs, clearly hesitant to offer more input after that rude chicken comment.

"Fine," I grumble to Michal, "but you had better nail the complex monologues and the emotional arc I'll be writing into that role."

With the casting complete, I study the members of this new, unexpected theater troupe. The superstar and his little sister. The diva's understudy. The loner. And me, the guy who ruined a school show. *Welp, Kennedy, we'll give it our best shot.*

KENNEDY

Hey, Calvin.
Haven't seen you in like a week.
What's going on?

> Not much
> Been busy

Doing what?
Come over today.
I need help picking NYC outfits

> Sorry, can't

Huh?
What's going on?
Are you mad I'm leaving?
Can we talk?

> Just busy, sorry
> Let's hang out soon for sure

CHAPTER 8

One week and a fabulous script later, we are ready to go. This brilliant piece of cinema will definitely convince Kennedy to stay, and it all begins here: our first flashback scene at Cone-y Island.

Michal and I are cramped into a booth on either side of Maia, who looks like a true star with her glittery dress and oversized sunglasses that cover half her face. I wear my Easter blazer, while Michal's hair is squished beneath a baseball cap that feels out of character for Kelvin Kenray, but what can you do? An enormous sundae sits on the table in front of her.

Our film crew, Jonah and Blake, occupy the seat across the table. The camera in Blake's hands has a few dings on one side, and there's a large piece of gray duct tape stretching across the top holding it all together. This camera has seen some things, but

Blake promised it can take a better-quality video than any phone ever could.

Sarah's boyfriend, Anthony, sits with his arm around my sister in the booth behind them, awaiting their entrance. He has a construction-paper mustache taped to his face and wears his grandfather's fedora, while Sarah wears her regular clothes and says it's the best we're going to get. It's a good thing these two aren't major characters in this film.

"Action," Jonah calls as Blake pushes the little button on his beat-up camera.

The red light glares at me and my stomach flutters. This is the first time I've performed since the last time I performed, and we all know how that went. Blake gently nods behind the camera. *Breathe, Calvin. Breathe,* he silently instructs, so I do.

I take a deep breath, turn to Maia, and recite the lines I memorized last night: "Another great performance, Melody Monarchy. Don't you love local small-town theater?"

"It's the best," Melody agrees. "And what a fun cast party this is. Ice cream! How nice."

Michal stuffs a spoonful of ice cream into her mouth. "Forsooth," she says, flashing the camera a fudge-covered grin.

My face reddens. That was definitely not in the script. Fingers crossed Blake can fix that with the wizard editing skills he claims to have.

Maia-as-Melody pushes through like a pro. "You know, I can't take all the credit for this show's success. You two really put the *support* in supporting cast. What would I be without you?" Maia removes her sunglasses so she can look from Michal to me with fondness, revealing a face caked in makeup. I've never seen such a vivid combination of reds and blues, and her drawn-in eyebrows look about as real as Anthony's paper mustache. Blake nearly drops the camera in surprise.

Michal's line is next, but she's so distracted by her sundae that I don't think she remembers we're filming. This, friends, is why you don't give a role with this much nuance to an amateur.

"That's a really good question," I say, having Johnny take Kelvin's line. "Something you might want to think really long and hard about."

Maia's phone rings, and she answers. "Hello? . . . Uh-huh . . . Uh-huh . . . Uh-huh . . . Ok. Thank you." Maia hangs up.

"Who was that?" I ask, pretending it wasn't secretly Sarah one booth over.

"Broadway," she replies.

"Gosh," I say. "What did they want?"

Melody gulps. "Me."

My eyes water, because this scene suddenly feels far too real. "They're not the only ones," I have Johnny say.

"Excuse me," Anthony says, approaching our table. "Aren't you Melody Monarchy, star of *Girl Scout Cookies: The Musical*? I'm a famous agent, and wow, do I have an offer for you!" His paper mustache flaps as he speaks. Sarah snorts, and I'm pretty sure Anthony and Maia are fighting laughter too.

"Girl Scout Cookies?" Michal mutters, finally paying attention to the scene. "I didn't get any cookies."

"You didn't order any cookies," snaps the angry tattooed server behind the counter. "And if the rest of you don't order something soon, you're gonna need to pack it up and get outta here."

The little red light is still taking it all in, so I do what any second- or at least third-in-command would do and yell, "Cut!" Blake stops rolling. I glare at each of our actors and hope my eyebrows are even half as frightening as Maia's. "What was that?"

Maia pulls out the crumpled script tucked away

on her lap. "I think you mean, what is *this*? I really hope you're a better vocal coach than script writer."

"What's wrong with my script?"

"It's a little clunky," Blake says. Which isn't especially constructive criticism in my opinion.

"Maybe what this story needs is an actually cool character," Sarah pipes up. "Like Kelvin Kenray's sister, Cierra."

"Are you volunteering to audition?" I ask her. "Or should we get Maia's squawking stuffed chicken to play the extra part?"

Sarah rolls her eyes. Anthony can't decide if he wants to defend or laugh at my scowling sister.

In desperation I turn to Jonah, who's let the scene wander so far off track. Doesn't he realize how important this film is?

He shrugs. "Honestly, Calvin, I don't think this is what Kennedy needs." His soft tone is sorrowful, but his comment still stings. "What is this supposed to inspire?"

The cashier replies, "A new charge-by-the-hour policy."

I roll my eyes at the man and turn back to my friends. "Maybe you'd get it if you were paying attention."

Maia laughs. "Paying attention? It's not particularly subtle."

"Kinda like your makeup," I push back.

"It's called Hollywood glam."

"Have you ever seen a movie before?"

She brings a hand up to her face, and I detect a hint of sadness beneath all the foundation.

"Look," I say before anyone can quit. "The point of the scene is that Kelvin Kenray is a nobody without Melody Monarchy. Nobody saw him before she did. And yeah, maybe they only notice him now because he's standing in the far edge of her spotlight, but what do you think is going to happen to him if she exits stage left and her spotlight turns off forever? He owes her everything. He needs her, and I need Kennedy to see that."

I swear I hear crickets in the seconds that follow. Everyone stares at me with a spectrum ranging from pitying smirks to wide-eyed concern.

"Okay, folks," Blake says in such an authoritative voice that even the cashier stops to stare. You'd almost think *he* was the director. "Listen up. We're gonna shoot it from the top—"

"Like heck you are," the cashier grumbles, but Blake snaps his fingers at him without even looking, and the cashier falls silent. My mouth drops open at how tough Blake seems right now. Like Sandy at the end of *Grease*. Maybe that's why he's always wearing black.

"And this time, Michal, you're going to say your lines or you're out." He turns to Maia. "You're going to tone down the makeup." To Sarah and Anthony, "You are going to take this seriously." He finally spins to face our director. "And Jonah, you will step up or go home."

Jonah carefully considers these options. I honestly can't tell what he'll decide. I thought he got weird after I fell off the stage, but that's nothing compared to how he's been since the last day of school. I almost had my friend back the other day in the basement, but I'm afraid he's gone again.

His eyes meet mine. "Cal. Kelvin isn't . . . You aren't . . . You're . . ." He looks away and sighs. "I'm gonna miss her too." More loudly, he continues: "From the top in five." He turns to Maia and waves a pretend washcloth over his face.

"Fiiiiiine," she grumbles, pushing through to the restroom. Sarah follows to help.

"So you *can* direct." Blake tips an invisible hat at Jonah. "Way to show up."

"Like how you showed up out of nowhere and suddenly think you're one of us?" Jonah snaps back. "Do you even know Kennedy?"

"Whoa, whoa, whoa," I say before things fall apart again. "Can anyone truly *know* Kennedy?" The rhetorical question seems to work. We sit in silence until Maia and Sarah return, Maia with a makeup-free face. "Better?"

We nod our approval as Michal drops her spoon and swipes her chocolate-covered lips with the back of her hand. "I'm gonna need another sundae before the next take," she announces. Her eyes turn up to me expectantly. And I thought Kennedy was a diva.

Five dollars and thirty-five cents later, I'm tempted to ask Maia how many stuffed chickens she has, but before I can, Blake has pushed the little red button and Jonah calls out, "Action!"

CHAPTER 9

That night, a text from Jonah lights up my phone: Sorry about today. Let me make it up to you. Free next Saturday?

Sure, I quickly text back, hoping it'll be okay with Mom and Dad.

Turns out Jonah's aunt Dorothy promised him four tickets to a big-time city show as a gift for his upcoming bar mitzvah. The sequel to *The Phantom of the Opera* is playing in Boston! My parents won't love the idea, but maybe I can convince them if I assure them we'll be responsibly chaperoned.

Who else are you inviting besides me and Kennedy? I ask Jonah. I'm not sure how I'll manage to hang out with her for a whole day and not let a hint of our surprise slip.

Jonah replies, Not Kennedy. Maia. It'll give us

inspiration for the film. If Jonah thinks we're going to come anywhere near the production values of *Phantom 2*, he's overestimating our skills and budget, but I don't argue. I've never seen a Real Show before.

And Blake? I text back, since he's the other key player in our film.

There's a long pause. What do you think? he finally responds.

Definitely. We need all the inspiration we can get. I can invite him now!

K.

Eight days, two choir practices, and a thirty-minute train ride to Boston later, we are here. "North Station. Last stop," the conductor announces.

We rise from the cranberry vinyl seats: Maia and me on one side of the aisle, Jonah and Blake on the other. I thought maybe the ride would be enough to break their tension, but I didn't hear a peep from across the aisle, while getting quite the earful from Maia. I'm sure I've learned everything about her: best friend who moved away; half a heart locket round her neck; pair of rowdy brothers whose passion for soccer has usurped her parents' attention; mom who always wanted to be a fashion designer but settled on being a realtor and the school shows' volunteer costumer; rebellious grandma who relocated the entire family from Arizona to Massachusetts before Maia was even born amid some sort of scandal that probably would've been really interesting to hear about if I hadn't been peeking over at Jonah and Blake, wondering why they can't even try to get along.

As we shuffle down the aisle single file, nerves shake my stomach. I've never been to the city without a supervisor before, and if you ask my mom, I still haven't. Sarah's here. Wink, wink. My sister dropped us off at the train station back home and said, "Tell Mom I'm with you the whole time, or you're dead." Then she drove off to spend the day with Anthony. Win-win. This kind of plan would normally freak me out, but with Maia telling her mom the exact same story, there's nothing to worry about. Everyone knows three Bible Study kids wouldn't lie.

"Oh, hey," I call to Maia, handing her my phone. "Take my picture, will you?" I pause in the train aisle and put on my best *small-town hopeful with big-city dreams* face as Maia snaps the shot. I send it to Sarah so she can send it to my parents so they'll think my sister and I are together. Then I take one of Maia for Sarah to send to Mrs. Ruiz.

Jonah laughs. "You are so ridiculous, Cal." Despite having to sit next to Blake, he seems more relaxed than I've seen him in weeks. This alone feels worth lying to my parents for.

We exit onto a long, gray platform. It's a little after noon, and the speckled concrete almost glistens in the warm sunlight.

"T's this way," Blake says at the same moment that Jonah suggests, "Let me call an Uber." One points toward the subway as the other faces the exit to the street. They both freeze and glare at each other.

Maia takes the opportunity to push between them and take charge. "Walking will save us money. One of my cousins lives in Roxbury, so I come into the city all the time. Trust me."

Jonah and Blake shrug and follow, so I do the same.

"I used to live here too," Blake murmurs, filling in another piece of his mysterious history, though I don't think anyone hears but me.

We exit into the city streets, and my nostrils are immediately greeted by the scent of Dunkin' and gym sneakers. I lift my hand to shield my eyes from the glimmer of the sparkling skyscrapers that must be hundreds of stories tall.

I'm brought back to street level as a bright purple duck-tour boat rushes by. The tourists on board use little plastic kazoos shaped like duck bills to quack at me as they zip past. Everyone has somewhere to be, and they're all wearing Red Sox gear to get there. Can't say I'm a fan of the game, but I love a good costume.

"Calvin," Maia calls from farther down the sidewalk.

"Coming," I say, rushing to catch up. Can you imagine the earful Mom and Dad would give Sarah if I got left behind? Not to mention the "bad parent" rumors that would ripple through the church community and forever sully my parents' reputations.

We cut through a few side streets that I'd never be able to find again on my own. Focus, Calvin. Focus.

Up ahead, the sound of music fills the air. Not like the monk-understudy hills-are-alive *Sound of Music*. This is the ground-thumping-with-bass-that-makes-you-wish-you-could-dance kind of music. There's a high-pitched "WOO!" and another and another.

Before I can wonder if this is the *Phantom 2* crowd hyping up before the show, we turn onto a street that's jam-packed with people and rainbows. So. Many. Rainbows.

Maia, Blake, and Jonah all stop in their tracks to take in the scene. I'm glad I'm not the only one in awe.

A flatbed truck slowly rolls past, carrying at least ten women in sparkling gowns with giant colorful hair, moving along with the thunk of the bass. Unlike me, these ladies can dance. Most of the crowd takes pictures or waves rainbow flags. They're all cheering. It's a parade. A rainbow parade. A—

Wait.

A.

Minute.

I look at the platform heels on one of the dancers. They're almost exactly like the ones on the album cover of *Kinky Boots*, one of the soundtracks I'm only able to listen to when I'm at Kennedy's house, far from Mom's overprotective ears.

"Are these rainbows . . . ?" I lean in toward Maia to ask.

"Celebrating God's covenant with Noah," Maia finishes. I can't tell if she's kidding until she snorts at her own joke.

My heart is racing. If my parents find out where we are . . . what we're watching . . .

Maia pulls out her phone to capture the float before it drives away.

"Don't post that," I beg.

"Calvin, it's called Pride for a reason. There's nothing to be afraid—"

"They're not celebrating God," I say, louder than I mean to.

A couple of heads turn to me, judging me. "Who brought the Bible thumper?" somebody asks.

Luckily the song changes and the next group of paraders approaches, pulling everyone's attention away from me before I can reach a fall-off-the-stage level of panic.

"Relax, Calvin," Maia whispers. "It's fine."

"I didn't mean to be *un*fine," I begin to explain. "Because I'm not. Unfine with it. I've listened to the whole *Kinky Boots* cast album on low volume."

Maia snorts again. "Wow, you really are an ally."

I turn as red as the top stripe of everyone's rainbow flags. I have that pre-audition jitter in my stomach, and I just want to get out of here. But it's not because I'm unfine, Maia. In fact, if my parents saw how fine I was right now, they would be mad.

I glance over to Jonah and discover he's looking right at me. His eyes dart away before I can gather whether he is fine or unfine.

My breath feels shallow as I return my attention to the parade. A bunch of men shimmy past, some wearing those kinky boots, others sporting funky tutus. A million different body shapes and colors, all dancing as one. And so many bare stomachs. Muscular ones and floppy ones and everything in between. The crowd "woo"s. I wonder why we're still here and what my parents would think and how come I can't stop staring.

I feel a hand on my back, and my body stiffens. I whip around; it's Blake. "You okay?" he asks.

"Totally fine," I say, staring into his eyes to show him how one hundred percent totally fine I am, despite what Maia thinks.

His lips curl into that crooked smile. "Good," he says. "Me too."

"I just don't want to be late," I say. "For the show."

Blake seems to understand. He taps Jonah, then Maia, and tips his head. "Let's go."

Maia leads the way again, Jonah right behind her. Blake brings up the rear, placing his hand on my shoulder to help guide me through the crowd. He doesn't let go until several blocks later, once we've lost the parade and found the theater. Even after he releases me, I still feel the imprint of his sweaty hand on my shoulder blade.

CHAPTER 10

Okay, so *Phantom 2* doesn't make a whole lot of sense. I thought the Phantom was supposed to be the bad guy. Maybe it would've helped if I actually saw the first one. I've listened to the original *Phantom* cast album, but I mostly stick to the tracks that don't make me blush knowing Mom is in the next room. I probably missed some nuances.

Still, I stand with my friends as the cast members take their bows, soaking in the adrenaline that's coursing throughout the majestic, appropriately-named Opera House.

The lush curtains drop as the room brightens, re-illuminating the most ornate building I've ever seen. Every surface is covered in gold flourishes and luxurious red velvet, except of course the ceiling, which is covered with painted baby angels hovering above us all. They remind me of church choir, and I wonder how I'm possibly going to sing God's praises tomorrow morning after the things I've seen today.

We slowly shuffle through the crowd toward the exit. I hug my first official Playbill tightly to my chest as I try to process the mysterious, beautiful spectacle we've all witnessed.

"What'd you think?" Blake breathes into my ear.

"I don't even know where to begin," I marvel.

"Me either," he says with a laugh.

Step by step, we slink along the crowded corridor, down the grand staircase and beneath the crystal chandeliers. Finally, we find ourselves outside.

"To the train?" Maia asks, ready to lead us back through the Pride-filled streets.

"Not yet," Jonah says. "I have a surprise. This way." I'm not sure if I can handle any more surprises today, but we all follow Jonah into a nearby alley, where a crowd is gathered in front of a nondescript beige door protected by a velvet red rope. If it weren't for the gathering crowd, I don't think I would've noticed the door at all.

"Trust me," Jonah says to me in particular because I'm the scarediest of the group.

I trust him for almost five minutes before starting

to lose my patience. What is Mom gonna say when we're ten hours late because we stopped to stand outside a door that never opened?

Except suddenly, it opens.

The folks around me clap and scream as the actor who played the Phantom emerges. He has a square jaw and the whitest teeth I've ever seen. His dark hair is slicked back, except for a stray swoop across his forehead.

Phones fly out: flashing, filming, snapping, streaming. He starts making his way along the queue, leaning in for selfies, signing autographs. He's followed by like six other actors, including the lady who played Christine.

Everyone is so happy, but as the Phantom gets closer to us, his approach feels more like a small crisis to me. You're not supposed to meet your heroes, especially when they just performed their hearts out in a show so professional that you can't even pretend to understand the plot, and here you are, so pathetic that you can't even put a shoe on a girl without falling off the stage. What would I even say to him?

When he reaches my friend group, he pulls Jonah into a hug like they're old friends. Jonah leans in to take a selfie of the two of them, and whispers something. The Phantom and Jonah both glance toward me. Did Jonah tell him about the Incident? Why would he do that?

The Phantom smiles at me. "Hi there."

"Uhhhhhh." I breathe through my nose. *Say something, you fool.* I inhale and tell the Phantom, "Whatever Jonah told you about me was a joke. Unless it was nice. Then it may be true. Also, you're a really good actor, and I should know because Kennedy Carmichael's my best friend. From the Girl Scout commercials, you know? But you're better. And like a thousand times better than I could ever be."

He takes in my words with a thoughtful expression.

"Oh wow, you're scary," I add.

He throws his head back and laughs.

I feel so worthless and embarrassed. I need to get out of here. I want to run, but there's a forbidden parade on the loose, and I'll never make it to the train without getting caught up in those funky grooves that I'm so fine with, which my parents can never know about.

"What's your name, kid?" the Phantom asks. I'm not sure what crime against theater I've committed, but if I tell him my real name, I'm sure my days on the stage will be officially over.

As I'm trying to decide what fake name to use, Jonah answers for me: "That's Calvin."

What is he doing?! At least I can throw out a fake last name—

Until Maia goes, "Calvin Conroy."

I throw a metaphorical rose onto the grave of my theatrical career.

The Phantom lifts the rope and beckons for me to come under it. This is exactly what he did to Christine in the play.

I shake my head No Thank You, but Blake pushes me forward. What is the matter with my friends today? It's clear I have no choice, so I duck under the red rope barrier, bracing myself. *Don't cry. Don't cry.*

The Phantom calls over the rest of his castmates to join us. The crowd groans as the actors skip the line and gather round the Phantom and me. "You're a riot," he says in the most unscary, un-phantom-like tone. "And one day, this'll be you."

"Forsooth," Maia says, and I almost don't hate her for it. I feel oddly amazing.

Christine pats my arm. "How about a picture?"

Maia is on it, her phone already out. Christine and the Phantom each place a hand across one of my shoulders, and the other cast members squeeze in. I think I'm dead or dreaming, because somehow, me being me has led to this, the most magical moment of my life.

My Playbill facing out for the camera, I put my hand on my hip and pop a pose.

"They loved you, Cal," Jonah says on the train home. "I totally knew they would."

"Thank you," I tell Jonah. I turn to Blake, who pushed me under the ropes. "Thank you," I add. Finally, I twist toward Maia by my side. "Thank you." I cannot stop zooming in and out of the picture she took. This is the single greatest photograph in the history of pictures of me. There's no way I am not printing this out a hundred times and putting it in every single frame in our living room.

I glance back up at Jonah, still in a bit of a haze. "How do you even know the Phantom?"

Jonah laughs. "My aunt knows him. It's how she got us tickets so quickly."

"Kennedy would've loved this," I say wistfully. I feel kind of bad about leaving her out—and maybe worse that this is the first time I've had this thought all day.

He shrugs. "NYYAPA sponsors a bunch of field trips to Broadway shows. She'll get to see plenty of musicals that way. And I specifically wanted *you* to see this one with me." He bumps his shoulder against mine. "It's okay for you to do stuff for yourself, Cal. Without her."

Before I can figure out how to respond to that, a text from Kennedy buzzes across my screen: Where are you?

Obviously, we can't tell her about the surprise or where we were today, but this kind of trip is exactly what we need to make our summer epic and convince her to stay. She's not even gone, and I already miss her so much. At home, I lie in my reply. What's up?

Sarah picks Blake and me up at the train station for the five-minute ride home. "Have a nice double date?" she teases.

I can feel my cheeks go numb with embarrassment as I think of the parade we saw today.

"Calvin met the entire cast," Blake says, ignoring her comment. He's learning.

"How'd he manage that?" Sarah asks. "Did you fall *onto* the stage this time?"

"Ha ha, very funny," I grumble.

Her voice softens as we pull into the driveway. "I know you like drama, but . . ." She nods toward our front door. "Be careful with this one."

I look up, and there on our front stoop is Kennedy.

I stuff the Playbill behind my back as both Blake and I exit the car, but it's too late. She knows.

CHAPTER 11

"So, you have a new best friend now?" Kennedy nods toward Blake as he slinks across the front yard toward his own house.

"I have a new friend," I correct, crossing my arms and accidentally flashing my Playbill in front of her face.

"And he's into theater?"

"Um, yeah. Kinda."

She holds out her phone. "It's funny." She chuckles, so I do too. Two best friends, sharing a laugh about a misunderstanding. "Maia's also a big fan of the theater." She slowly turns the screen to reveal a post: the picture of me with the cast of *Phantom 2*.

"She posted it?" I ask, mortified—and worried about what else she may have shared.

"I'm not gone yet. But I am done being ignored."

She stuffs her phone back into her bag. Kennedy's a great actress, but the water glistening in her eyes looks a little too real. "So I'm leaving. Early."

"Kennedy, you can't be serious!" I protest.

"Give me a reason to stay."

I'm practically speechless. Why are surprises so hard? "Me! I need you!"

"You sure have a messed-up way of showing it, Cal. We had a good run. Like a *Wicked*-good run. But I've decided to do NYYAPA's summer theater program, so the next time you're in the *real* big city, you and your new friends can find me in the spotlight. Catch me at the stage door."

Her shoulder thwacks against mine as she pushes past. It stings in more ways than I can count.

She says over her shoulder, "I'm done letting you bring me down."

"Bring you down? What are you talking about?"

She stops and slowly turns to face me. Her eyes lock with mine. "You're the reason I'm moving, Calvin."

"*What?*" I'm sure I misheard because that doesn't make any sense.

"When you fell off that stage, I realized I couldn't grow into my potential in this town, so my parents and I made a choice. Now I'm leaving. So, thank you. Really."

Is it possible for all the air to be sucked out of the room when you're standing outside?

My performance as the Footman was so awful that one of my only friends is literally moving out of town. I thought Jonah acting standoffish was the worst of it. I thought that despite it all, Kennedy was at least trying to understand, sending me video clips of famous comedians and clowns. All this time she was actually planning her escape from me.

This is the meanest thing anyone has ever said to me. I want to sob, and the only way to stop myself is to say the meanest thing back: "I'd fall off that stage again if it got you out of here faster."

She flinches, and I hope she feels an ounce of my pain.

"And Maia loved the show today. It was a pleasure to see it with a *real* actress."

"A real *understudy*," Kennedy retorts, "with remarkably low standards. I guess she doesn't care if tagging someone with only fifteen followers makes her page look pathetic."

"That's not fair! I'd have more followers if my parents weren't so concerned about my privacy." Possibly.

"Whatever, Calvin," she says. "I don't care. I'm done." She spins around and storms off. I wonder if she's picturing the same cape fluttering behind her that I am. Who am I kidding? Of course she is. She taught me everything I know about dramatic exits. She taught me everything I know about Broadway musicals and inside jokes and yes, even friendship. What have I done?

"Kennedy, wait!" I call out, but she's already halfway down the sidewalk.

I barge into the house to find Mom and Dad waiting for me, side by side like soldiers. I swear sometimes they take this General thing way too seriously. Sarah settles onto the couch behind them, popping open a can of soda and flipping on the TV.

"How was the show?" Mom pipes up.

"Um, very moving," I say with a sniff, hoping they haven't noticed the small twin rivers working their way down my cheeks.

"Did Maia get a nice picture with the cast like that one Sarah sent to us?"

"Just me," I say. It stings that my mom sounds

almost proud of me for once and it's only because she wants to one-up Mrs. Ruiz.

"Why wasn't Kennedy with you?" my dad asks in a stern tone.

"We only had one more ticket." I quickly swipe beneath my eyes. "And Jonah chose Blake." As if that would ever happen, but it feels easier to blame Jonah than to hear my parents express more concern about my friendship with Blake.

Dad tilts his head a little. "Are you—"

"Leave him alone," Sarah snaps in a protective voice that shocks us all. I wonder how much she heard between Kennedy and me before letting herself inside. "He needs a minute."

Actually, Sarah, I need at least five hundred twenty-five thousand six hundred minutes, but I salute your effort. I'll take what I can get.

I race to my room, lock my bedroom door behind me, and let a sob escape. Kennedy didn't mean it. How could she? I look up—and catch a ghost lurking outside my window.

"AHH!" I scream before realizing it's only Blake.

He taps the glass twice as if I haven't nearly died from the shock of noticing him already. I switch on the lights before throwing open the window and screen. Blake easily hoists himself up onto the sill, which probably isn't as easy as it looks even though my room's on the first floor. A small clump of dirt drops from his shoe onto my floor as he swings one leg inside, followed by the other.

"What are you doing here?" I ask, quickly brushing the tears from my eyes because I can't have him think that I am literally crying all the time even though I clearly am.

"You and Kennedy weren't exactly quiet as I was walking away. Are you okay?"

I cross my arms and lower myself onto my bed. Who is this guy? Always asking if I'm okay. Giving me his yearbook. Knowing when to hold me up and when to push me forward into the greatest moment of my life. I don't get it. "Why are you being nice to me?"

"Because I'm your friend." He slides the screen shut and takes a seat by my side.

There's a long pause as I try to figure out how to express what I mean. "How do you always know what to do?"

Blake breaks into a smile. "Years of therapy," he says, as if that's as normal as going to school or the grocery store, and maybe it is. "My dad struggles with anxiety, and it's affected all of us. It can be really intense sometimes. It's why we moved out of the city. My parents hoped living somewhere quieter would help, but . . ."

He shakes his head. I'm not totally sure that I'm following all this, but it's obvious that things have been hard for him.

"Anyway," he continues, "when you fell off the stage . . ."

Oh no.

He puts a hand on my knee. "I saw something I recognized. I wanted to tell you that you were going to be okay. And I knew I wanted to be your friend."

As I fight to hold in my tears, I accidentally make a blubbering noise, making it even more obvious that I'm crying. Instead of judging me, Blake leans back and reaches over to my nightstand to grab me a tissue. I don't say it, but I miss his hand on my knee. It means so much that somebody cares—and not in the mortified Mom way or the admonishing Dad way or the teasing Sarah way or the avoidant Jonah way or the using-me-to-get-the-church-solo Maia way or the running-off-to-a-more-promising-career Kennedy way.

"No pressure," Blake says as I unload a round of boogers into the tissue, "but do you want talk about it? That night?"

I haven't wanted to talk about it since it happened, but something's different now. I almost place my hand on Blake's knee before second-guessing myself and resting it in the space between us. With a deep breath, I begin: "Okay, so you're standing on the stage, right?"

KENNEDY

Can we talk? I'm so sorry for what I said.
And I'm sorry I fell off the stage.

Something weird is happening, Kennedy
I wish I could tell you what, but I can't

I really can't

It almost feels like

I don't know

Please don't leave now

I need you

Seen.

CHAPTER 12

"It's showtime," Ms. Clarkson says to the group, smacking her dusty hands together. Maia and I have gathered with the rest of the youth choir in the church lobby for our first official performance.

As my fellow holy vocalists and I enter the church in a rigid double file line that would make the General proud, the oversized sculpture of Jesus above the altar looks down at me, arms stretched out. He twinkles in the rainbow light from the stained glass windows, looking way too much like a parade I wasn't supposed to see yesterday. I glance at Maia to my right. Not like I wasn't fine with it.

I catch my parents and sister seated in the front pew as we march past: one brimming with excitement about my pending church choir debut, one unreadable, and one making goo-goo eyes at Anthony from across the church. Not like being fine with it *means* anything, I throw in their direction.

Rainbow Jesus says nothing, but I know what He's thinking, and I stumble, stepping on the navy robe that's at least two sizes too big. Ms. Clarkson told everyone they had to wear adult sizes since most of the teens can't fit in the bright blue kid robes. Unfortunately for Maia and me, the costumes eat us alive.

When we arrive at the folding chairs that have been set up in the front, I shuffle into the first row along with Maia and the other short folks. Ms. Clarkson settles onto the piano bench, her back to us. She cracks her knuckles and places her hands upon the keys.

As the first chord rings, everyone in the room rises. *Call 911!*, a voice in my head shrieks, recalling the last time an audience stood before me. My stomach squeezes as the opening lines of "Gather Us In" spill from my lips. Father Paul and the rest of the Holy Cast enter without a hitch, and I get through the whole song without falling down or making a scene. That's how you know it's not Real Art.

It's not until Father Paul stands behind the pulpit and says, "Let us pray" that my heart begins to race.

There's so much on my mind that it's hard to decide where to even begin.

Dear God, it's me, Calvin Conroy. So, I don't know if You were listening yesterday, but it turns out that Kennedy's moving because I fell off the stage, and then I made everything even worse by saying something horrible. Please let her forgive me and help us convince her to stay. And if homemade films can win Oscars—I don't know, just a thought. Anyway, I don't mean to be a burden, but if You have another moment, there's actually something else too. About Blake. He's my new friend who lives next door, but I guess You already know that . . .

Blake stayed for like an hour last night, listening to me talk. He never even stopped me once to take a selfie or sing a song or check his phone. *So anyway, why'd You choose to show me that parade on the same day Blake came over and made me feel—*

"Psst," Maia says, kicking my brown loafer with her clunky black heel.

"Ahhhh!" I scream. Half the parish jumps.

Everyone around me has gathered the sheet music for the next song as if they haven't memorized it from years of church attendance, and now they're all looking at me. I lunge forward to grab mine, and of course the bottom of my robe is caught on my foot because it's like a mile too long. I pop forward into a music stand. It clatters to the floor, and the other half of the parish jumps.

I listen to Blake's voice in my mind as he encourages me to *Breathe.*

After I've righted the music stand and Ms. Clarkson has shifted her glare back to the black-and-white keys, I notice Jesus nailed to the cross, and I swear He's frowning. Did He always look like that, or did He hear my partial prayer?

I didn't even say anything. I mouth along to the music while engaging in a staring contest with a statue. I know his sculpted abs shouldn't remind me of Pride, but why do the rainbows of the stained glass windows look so familiar and why am I thinking about Blake again? I try to shake the thought from my mind with a literal shake of my head. This is totally not the choreography, so I sway a little to make it seem like part of the number, which reminds me of Kennedy, who would add a little pizzazz to any routine to make it her own. I shimmy my shoulders in her honor.

"What are you doing?" Maia whispers as I continue swaying. I have to make this look purposeful. I throw my hands over my head and clap. Okay, I need to sell it better. I clap again. And again. And again. I almost feel like I belong in a production of *Joseph and the Amazing Technicolor Dreamcoat*. Maybe there's room for artistry in church choir after all.

Maia is giving me some serious what-the-fudge eyes, but if I'm ever going to be a star like the Phantom predicted, I need to be a leader. So I lean toward Maia and whisper, "What would the soloist do?" and somehow it works. The next time I smack my hands together, Maia joins. Okay. Let's do this.

I push up my enormous flappy sleeves and turn to face the rest of the choir, taking over as unofficial bandleader. I swing my arms in time to the song, trying to conduct my flummoxed choir mates, who are absolutely not clapping along, but here we are, making beautiful Sunday morning music.

Until talon-like hands clench me from behind. I shriek. Ms. Clarkson has risen from her perch. Everyone stops singing.

I spin from her grasp, arms out, but that isn't the best idea when you're in a tight space and still stepping on a mile-too-long robe. My hand thunks the same music stand I toppled earlier. This time it pops forward with the zest of the Holy Spirit, flying onto the altar and knocking over a candle that falls in slow motion as the flame brushes Father Paul's arm.

He lights up faster than a Christmas tree. The Lord is with him, though, as he whips off the robe and begins beating it against the floor.

My chest tightens. I feel dizzy. I need to get out of here.

The last thing I hear as I run down the aisle and out the door is my dad bellowing, "The wine! Use the wine!" and my mom shrieking, "Calvin, get back here!" Um. Pass!

Another star performance by Calvin Conroy. Thank you, folks. No autographs, please.

I explode out of the church, cross the parking lot, and take off down the sidewalk. I stop once to pull the robe off over my head and stuff it into a dumpster. If the police are looking for me, it'll be pretty easy to trace a description of "small boy in an adult-sized robe that hasn't been washed in years."

My legs are burning because I'm not a runner or even an exerciser if I can avoid it, but ten minutes later, I've reached my safe space: Jonah's house.

Forsooth, I hope he's home.

CHAPTER 13

When I poke my head into his bedroom, Jonah is facing a mirror with his eyes closed, speaking Hebrew words I don't understand. The sunny yellow stripes of a dozen Playbills beam down on me from the wall behind him where they're framed in perfect rows. He holds a crinkled cluster of papers tightly to his chest.

"Hey," I say, sorry to break the actor's focus.

His eyes pop open, and he fumbles with the papers, embarrassed. Why he'd be ashamed is beyond me. I can't even recall a few lousy lines in English without falling off a stage. Jonah will be reciting a whole section of the Torah in Hebrew. Even though he said he doesn't have to memorize it, he wants to.

"Aren't you supposed to be at church?" He rests

the sheets on his dresser beside the *Phantom 2* Play-bill, which hasn't made it onto the Wall of Fame yet.

"I don't know if there *is* a church anymore," I reply, glancing over my shoulder as if the fire could have followed me here.

My phone buzzes alive, and I pull it out to find a text from Sarah: OMG Calvin. I'm dying.

"Dying!" I shout out, nearly dropping my phone as Jonah exclaims, "What?!"

Another message comes through: Fire's out. Mom says get home now.

I quickly reply, Is Dad alive?

Obviously, she returns, followed by some expressive emojis: flame, glass of wine, and praying hands.

I'm relieved everyone made it out, but there's no way I'm going home right now. As soon as I get there, they'll ask me why I did what I did, and that's a big None of Their Business.

"You going to tell me what's going on?" Jonah says, losing patience. I can see the frustration of not-knowing across his face, a feeling I know all too well.

I burst out, "Kennedy's moving away because I ruined her big scene—"

"She said that?"

"And after I fell, things changed between you and me. It was your big scene too, and I know I ruined it, and . . ."

"Cal." Jonah holds up a hand to stop me. "My big scene hasn't happened yet."

I don't know whether he's referring to his bar mitzvah or some other upcoming star turn, but it almost makes me feel hopeful. "Then what is going on with us? Nothing's been the same lately. You've . . ." I force myself to say it. "You've been pushing me away. And Kennedy too."

"It's complicated." His eyes lock with mine. "When you fell . . ." He stops, perhaps realizing that my worst moment is not the best place to begin. He tries again: "When we were in the city yesterday . . ." He trails off again. I wonder if he was as overwhelmed as I was. He releases a frustrated snort-sigh, and says, "You know, not everyone has the luxury of speaking their mind all the time."

"What does that mean?" I know that Jonah's often felt like an outsider in this town, in his temple, in our shows, but I never thought in our friendship. "You can tell me anything," I promise. "Unless it's that you're leaving too. I cannot make another movie."

"We can barely handle the first one," he says with a laugh. "Look, I'm sorry I hurt you. I didn't mean to push you away."

"What about Kennedy, though? You've been different with her too."

He sighs. "I didn't want things to change between us. Kennedy was one of my best friends. But when she . . ." He trails off.

"Kissed you?"

"You saw?"

I nod.

He grimaces. It's kind of a relief to know that Jonah wasn't ready for that kiss either. "It's hard to make a film honoring a friendship that feels like it's already over."

I hate that he feels this way. Maybe the love story is on pause, but Jonah and Kennedy share a bond that can't just disappear with one too-soon kiss. You don't costar in this many school productions and walk away without a permanent bond. When Kennedy's parents split up, Jonah talked her through the pain. When Jonah's mom started dating again, Kennedy character-studied the heck out of her boyfriends until we were laugh-crying, and the new men in Jonah's life didn't seem so scary anymore.

"We can save it," I say.

"The thing is, I don't know if I want to." He glances toward my wringing hands—perhaps wondering if they're available to hold? "But I know how much it means to you. The show must go on."

"Maybe you'll feel different by the time we're finished."

"Maybe," he says. "Maybe you will too." His lips curl into a smile that I cannot help but mirror. "But that's not why you were freaking out a minute ago, is it?" he asks. "What happened at church?"

"Oh, nothing. I set the priest on fire."

"You what?!" he exclaims as his mother enters the bedroom. She's a tall woman with a thick braid wrapped around the top of her head.

"Calvin?" she says, surprised to see me. "Your parents called and asked if you were here. I said no—"

"Thanks, Mrs. Franklin!" I say, glad to have a friend like Jonah with a generous mom who is willing to cover for me.

Except as it turns out, she said no because she didn't realize I was there. Michal had let me in. The next thing I know, Jonah's mother is insisting on driving me home.

"Text later?" Jonah asks, and I tell him of course.

When Mrs. Franklin drops me off, Mom and Dad are waiting for me at the front door.

"You're alive!" I exclaim, as if I've been searching for them ever since I hastily exited the church.

"Kitchen," Dad says, "now."

I trudge behind them, knowing better than to try escaping to my bedroom. They lead me to the small round table where we eat most of our family meals when the General isn't working late.

"Sit. Down," Dad growls.

I settle between them and brace myself for what's coming.

Dad uses his *project-for-the-folks-in-the-back* voice. Like, back of the yard. He's furious. "What were you thinking, Calvin? Were you? How could you be so careless—so selfish? You've embarrassed your mother and me in front of the whole church."

Of course this is about R number two—Reputation—and how Mom is going to explain this mess to her Bible Study friends. It feels like the night I ruined the play all over again, after we got home and my parents decided a scolding was better than the doctor-recommended therapy.

"Maia clapped too," I remind them.

"Did Maia knock over a candle and run from the church screaming?"

I didn't stay for the second half of the service, but I have to guess, "Probably not."

Mom sighs. "What are we going to do with you, Calvin?" The quiver in her voice is crystal clear. Dad may be mad, but Mom is heartbroken.

"Let us pray?" I suggest, extending a hand toward each of my parents.

They both seem reluctant, but eventually their hands fall into mine.

I bow my head and mutter the first thing that comes to mind. "Dear Lord, thank You for sparing all of our lives in the Great Church Fire. We ask forgiveness for destroying the priest's robe, which was a complete and total accident so not quite a sin that we must punish, but more of a humorous misunderstanding that we'll laugh about one day."

"Calvin . . ." Dad warns. He releases his grip.

"Amen," I finish, letting go of Mom's hand. Before they can ground me for the rest of the summer, I rise to my feet. "I feel so much better. Thank you both—"

"Stop," the General barks before I can scurry away. "We're not done with you yet."

"Thanks, Dad," I reply. "I'm not done with you, either."

He almost smiles. I think I'm saved until Mom slams both of her hands on the table and yells, "Enough."

Even Dad seems surprised. "Hon," he says, a mix of concern and confusion in his voice.

Mom ignores him and looks me in the eyes. "Grab your sister, and get in the car."

This can't be good.

CHAPTER 14

Father Paul sits behind his desk, which is cluttered with paperwork. On the other side of the desk, Mom, Dad, Sarah, and I are cramped together on four cold metal folding chairs. I've never been in the priest's office before, but it feels exactly like the principal's office—only smaller, and decorated with more pictures of Jesus, Mary, and sheep.

I wait for the punishment I know I deserve for setting a priest on fire.

"So, Calvin," Father Paul says, clasping his hands together. "Your mother tells me you've been having some problems."

I'm honestly surprised she shared her shame with anyone, let alone the guy in charge of our congregation. I wonder which problems she's mentioned, because last time I checked, I had about a dozen.

I take a guess that it's Kennedy. "My best friend's moving, and it's all my—"

The priest holds his hand up to silence me. My mouth snaps closed. "A friend leaving can be hard," he says with a sympathetic nod. "But you know who never leaves you?"

I nod and give an "Mm-hmm."

As the priest goes into a little monologue about Jesus, I allow my mind to wander to the people who *really* don't leave me. Jonah, for instance. He hasn't been with me quite as long as Kennedy, but I believe him when he said he was sorry about being distant lately. I've known Maia as a church acquaintance longer than anyone, and now we're finally almost actual friends. And then there's Blake. Brand new to my life, but I don't think anyone has ever understood me more than—

". . . Jesus," Father Paul wraps up the monologue and waits for me to reply.

Shoot. I glance up at my mother, who has been moved to the verge of tears by the priest's words. "Amen," I reply, hoping this does the job.

Sarah snorts but covers it up with a throat-clearing as Father Paul's eyes dart to her. When nobody says anything else, Father Paul rises and shimmies past a filing cabinet to reach a garment that's hanging on a hook. I recognize the frayed black fabric as the robe that I set aflame this morning. He drapes it across his desk. I catch a whiff of frankincense in the air, and I can't recall if the room always smelled like that or if holy robes give off a special scent when burnt to a crisp.

I'm sure my parents are cringing behind me. They hate being embarrassed (Reputation!) and lately that is one of my specialties.

"One hundred and fifty dollars," Father Paul says, and I'm confused as to why he thinks anybody would want to buy his old burnt robe.

My parents don't say anything, so I reply on their behalf. "No, thank you."

Father Paul laughs. "Cal," he says, and I scrunch up a bit. We aren't pals on a nickname basis. "I'm not selling it to you. I'm telling you what you owe."

My mouth falls open. "Where am I supposed to get one hundred and fifty dollars?"

Unfortunately, Father Paul isn't done: "And there's the matter of the robe *you* were wearing, which never found its way back to the church. Fifty dollars for that." I feel a moistness forming in my armpits, and if recent history has told me anything, there will soon be a special stench that frankincense and burnt robe may not be enough to hide.

I turn to my dad, the guy who can make this all go away with a quick trip to the ATM.

He knows exactly what I want, and he purses his lips. "Sorry, Cal. We don't have that kind of money to throw around. This one's on you."

I whip my head back to the priest. "Sir, Father Paul, I don't have that much money," I protest.

"You're lucky, my friend," the priest says with an irritating twinkle. "For God is with you today."

"I thought He was with me all the time," I reply.

This time, Sarah audibly guffaws.

Father Paul gives her some serious side-eye before returning to me. "True. And this time, He's decided to let you off easy."

"Thank you, God!" I bring my hands together, fingers pointed to the sky, and bow my head before the merciful deity who has just saved me two hundred bucks. "You won't regret this. I promise I'll never—"

"Not *that* easy," Father Paul says with a smirk. "For you will be blessed this summer with fifty hours of community service."

Mom clears her throat, looks at Sarah, and adds, "Each."

"Each?" Sarah cries. "I didn't set the church on fire. What the f—" She redirects mid-sentence: "What the heck did I do?"

"For starters," Mom says in a hushed voice as if Father Paul can't hear, "almost cursing in a priest's office."

"You've got to be kidding. That's entrapment!"

"Sorry, hon," Dad apologizes, sounding like he really means it. "But Calvin'll need a ride."

"So *this* is my fault too?" I push back. "Great."

"Conroys," Father Paul says before a family feud can begin right in the middle of his office. "Whose spirit couldn't benefit from sharing a little kindness?"

Sarah knows she's stuck, so she shuts her mouth, crosses her arms, and scowls at me as she rises from her folding chair. The curses I know she is hurling at me with her mind are enough to justify the community service and more, so I feel slightly less guilty.

"Now, before you go," Father Paul adds, "there's one more thing." I suspect he's about to hand over a bill for the candle I knocked over, but I'm not too worried about that. Mom's got a ton of candles at home so I can definitely grab him one of those. She'll never know.

"It's about the solo," Father Paul says, and my

back straightens. The summer solo. The reason Maia even joined our film for Kennedy. I told her I'd snag it for her, and this is my chance.

"I'm so glad you brought this up," I say, "because I've been thinking, and nobody deserves that solo more than Mai—"

"I'm giving it to you," he interrupts.

"YOUrrrr friend, Maia, you mean," I try.

He shakes his head. "Cal, your mom has told me about your little . . . mishap . . . at the school play, and now you've had another at church. I think that God can help. This solo is exactly what you need to face your fears and get you up on stage again."

Great. If Maia finds out about this, we're done for. She'll quit the movie and Kennedy will never know how much she means to me. My mind races for an excuse, but if this morning's events aren't enough to convince Father Paul that I'm a loose cannon, I'm not sure what would be.

Grasping, I say, "Could you still at least hold the auditions? To keep your options open."

Father Paul doesn't look especially convinced.

"Plus," I add, "I know everyone was really excited to try, so having the auditions will inspire everyone to be their best. It's for the sake of the choir. You can tell them it's going to me after you've heard the rest of them sing."

Finally, Father Paul nods. "Deal." He extends his hand.

"Peace be with you," I mumble as I shake his hand.

The old man erupts in laughter. My parents join. I hesitantly chuckle along. For Kennedy's sake, I hope Maia will think it's all as funny as we do.

CHAPTER 15

Something is off between my parents. Dad cannot get out of the church fast enough, and honestly, neither can I.

Mom quickens her step to keep up with him. "What?" she asks him with a hushed tone as if Sarah and I aren't right behind them. "We had to do something."

"We, or you?" he asks, matching her volume.

"If you heard what the girls were saying, you would understand where I'm coming from."

Dad throws open the car door and takes a deep breath. "If you stopped listening to them and started listening to *him*, maybe you would understand where *I'm* coming from."

Him Father Paul or *him* God? What is Dad saying? I don't think I've ever seen my parents disagree about anything before, and it's all my fault.

They don't speak on the ride home. They don't even put on their boring news radio. I want to text Sarah from the back seat, but I know she's furious at me too. Instead I pull out my phone and send a message to Kennedy: How did you know when your parents' marriage was in trouble? Crickets from my phone, crickets in the car. After an agonizing ten minutes, the car rolls to a stop in front of our house.

Four seat belts click. Four car doors open and slam behind us. Four family members go their separate ways without another word.

My phone buzzes as I head down the hallway toward my bedroom, and my heart jumps. I totally expected my parents to snatch my phone once we got home, but I guess community service, my sister's wrath, and an unwanted solo are punishment enough. I'm only a little disappointed to find a text from Jonah instead of Kennedy flash across the screen: What happened? How bad you grounded?

I reply, Community service. Ugh.

He sends me a series of exclamation points, followed by a You serious?

Well, I'm glad someone's excited. I send a trio of question marks.

Jonah's response pops up almost instantly: I'm

doing a whole summer of community service for my mitzvah project. We can do it together!

OMG! I type back. With a single text, Jonah has turned my punishment into funishment. Before I can choose an emoji that matches my excitement, the doorbell rings.

"Calvin," Mom calls from the entryway a moment later. "Visitor."

Who would be visiting me? Blake uses the window, and Jonah is texting me, which means . . .

The portrait of Jesus watches me nearly stumble as I run down the hall to greet Kennedy, who must've come back to tell me she's sorry. To tell me she didn't mean what she said last night. To tell me she's staying.

"Oh," I say as I see Maia standing in the doorway, still wearing the orange dress and clunky heeled shoes she had on beneath her choir robe at church this morning.

Maia's grin sinks along with mine. I wonder if she's already heard the secret of the solo, and she's here to quit the film.

Mrs. Ruiz hovers behind her, holding a steaming porcelain bowl that smells much more delicious than the PB&J I was planning on having for lunch.

"Calvin," she says, "What happened today?" Her voice rings with concern, but her piercing brown eyes are scanning me for scandal.

So this is why Maia's here.

"I got confused," I say, which feels true enough and much simpler than the mix of emotions that led me to setting the priest on fire. "I'm sorry I ruined the performance. I'm grateful Maia was there trying to help me save the show," I add, hoping to soften whatever trouble Maia's in with her family.

Mrs. Ruiz nods cautiously before following my mother inside to get the adult perspective. I really hope Mom keeps the secret of the solo like we agreed.

I usher Maia outside to the front lawn, closing the door behind me. "What's up?" I ask once I'm sure we're alone.

"You tell me," she says. "Calvin, you set a priest on fire after leading a clapping revolt." She studies me with the eyes of someone who really cares, which is not like the teasing Maia I know at all. "So, what is going on? Like really? Is it Kennedy?"

I don't know what to say. Maia wouldn't get it. She and Kennedy have never been close, and she's only doing this film to get the solo, which I've accidentally, secretly stolen from her. And even if she was perfectly okay with that parade yesterday, the thing with Blake is . . . absolutely nothing, and she might not understand why that's all it can ever be.

With no words, I flap my arms and gobble like that stuffed chicken she said should play Kelvin in the movie.

She laughs and shakes her head. "You are impossible. My parents are so mad I clapped along."

My face flushes. "Are you grounded?"

"After this visit, yeah."

"Your mom wanted the inside scoop first?"

Maia grimaces. "I won't say anything," she promises.

I gobble again, much more affectionately this time, and we both cackle.

"You are so weird," she says in a tone that means *You're okay, Calvin Conroy.*

"Thanks," I reply because she's okay too. She's more than okay, actually.

My smile droops. Kennedy film be danged, I need to tell Maia the truth. It's only fair. "Listen, Maia. About the solo . . ."

Before the words can spill from my mouth, my phone buzzes in my hand. I'm stunned to find a message from Kennedy: Your parents are fine.

Oh. My. God. How does she know? It doesn't even matter. Kennedy responded to my message, which means she still cares! I quickly reply: Are we?

She answers, I'll see you at Jonah's bar mitzvah.

"Jonah's bar mitzvah?" I mutter. "That's like a month away."

"Calvin?" Maia says, waving a hand in front of my face. "What were you saying about the solo?"

"Did she already leave?" I wonder out loud.

Maia frowns. "Kennedy? I thought you knew. I thought maybe that's why you . . ." She claps twice and sways to imaginary church music.

It's clear I have no idea what she's talking about, so she takes out her own phone and holds up the screen to face me. There's a post from Kennedy earlier this morning featuring a U-Haul truck in the driveway of her apartment complex. The caption reads, *Think of me* . . . I must have missed the post with everything that happened since last night. When she said she was leaving early, I didn't realize she meant *today*.

"No. No, no, no." I fall to my knees. I thought we had more time. How did she pack so fast? This doesn't make any sense.

"I'm sorry," Maia says, kneeling down to my level. "I know what it's like to lose a friend."

"I haven't lost her!" I push back.

"I know. But it won't be the same."

I can't even listen to the things Maia is saying. Kennedy answered my text, which means our friendship can be saved.

I know I should tell Maia the truth, but our movie will fix everything if only Kennedy can see how much Melody Monarchy means to her friends, and how many great things can be found right here at home.

I need her.

"Yeah, so about that solo." A bead of sweat drips down my cheek. "I, uh, still haven't found the perfect song for your audition, but I was thinking we could add another song or two to the film to get those vocals warmed up in the meantime. Sound good?"

She gobbles excitedly in a tone that means, *You're the best, Calvin Conroy*, and I wish it felt like the truth.

CHAPTER 16

"Presenting the sparkling superstar of small-town Massachusetts . . ." says Maia's grandmother with her faint Mexican accent. She's graciously wearing the costume pieces we provided: a men's blazer that eats her alive and an Uncle Sam hat that nearly covers her gray curly hair. ". . . Melody Monarchy! Of course," she can't help adding, "she is my beautiful grand-daughter, Maia Ruiz."

I glance to Blake, capturing the scene with his camera. I hope he knows this ad-lib will need to be removed in the final version.

Maia stands on the outdoor stage. She seems truly energized to be back out in the world after her one-week punishment. Her red, white, and blue outfit oozes America, much like Kennedy's did when she sang at our town's Fourth of July celebration two summers ago.

Of course, we've had to sneak onto the stage an hour before this year's festivities begin because sadly, we are not listed on the program. Still, there are maybe fifty fireworks pregamers gathering, eager for a good seat, including Jonah's mom sitting with Michal somewhere, and Maia's brothers, who are clustered around the stage. Her parents couldn't take the time off from work, she'd told us with a frown.

Jonah pushes Play on his phone and patriotic music fills the air.

"How y'all doin' tonight?" Maia says in the same fake country twang that Kennedy used two years ago. "America, I love you." She kisses two fingers and points them into the sky. "This one's for you."

One of the Ruiz brothers whoops. Maia smiles and begins to sing: "O beautiful, for spacious skies . . ."

My mouth falls open. This girl can *sing*. A hush falls over the green, and we all listen as Maia takes us on a journey over purple mountain majesties, through amber waves of grain, from sea to shining sea.

The music stops, and Melody Monarchy takes her bow. The pregamers burst into applause, everyone whistling and screaming and just loving America.

Maia has actual tears in her eyes. I honestly cannot tell if it's Maia or Melody Monarchy who says the line I threw together last night to make this scene fit into our movie: "Thank you all so much. This crowd. This town. Where would I be without you?"

Her brothers whoop again, as Melody Monarchy blows a kiss and takes her final bow.

"And cut," Jonah says, directing Blake to stop.

Maia runs over to her grandmother, who has already replaced her floppy costume cap with a broad, summery straw hat, and gives the old woman a giant embrace. After she helps her grandma off the stage, Maia quickly hugs the rest of her family before rejoining our little group.

"How was that?" she asks.

Better than Kennedy, I want to reply, but surely I'm misremembering. "Perfect," I say instead. "I wish Father Paul was here." This part is really true. If he heard that voice . . .

"We'll cook up something else special for him," Maia says, and the guilt throbs in my heart.

I point to the small hill behind us. "Shall we grab a seat for the fireworks?"

Maia lets her family know where we'll be, as Blake puts away the camera and scoops up the giant bag of popcorn he brought for us to share. I pick up the old ratty blanket that Mom keeps in the back of her car, and together we start our ascent.

"Can you hang out tomorrow?" Blake asks me as we walk. "I have something to show you."

"We have community service tomorrow," Jonah answers for me. I'm so glad we finally talked and he actually wants to spend time with me again.

"Community service?" Blake asks.

"I set the church on fire," I explain.

"Wait, what?"

"He didn't tell you?" Jonah asks, sounding almost proud.

"It was hilarious," Maia says.

"Are you okay?" Blake asks in a way that makes my cheeks burn.

I don't know how to tell him that thinking about his kindness while praying is what got me into this mess without hurting his feelings, so I nod and whisper, "Fine."

Halfway up the hill I spot our ride, Sarah, tucked behind a large tree that is the only place you *don't* want to sit for tonight's show. With her arms wrapped around Anthony, she's clearly not here for fireworks. At least not literal ones.

I whip my head away, because she's my sister, and I see the stepsisters from the school show, Ana and Estelle, approaching us from the other side. One wears stripes, the other stars.

"That was amazing, Maia," Estelle gushes. "I guess you're going for lead next year, huh?"

Maia smiles. "Hope so."

The stepsisters turn to Jonah. They're a year younger than us, and their crush on the man behind the prince is not a secret. "We heard about Ken," Ana says sympathetically as if that's her nickname. Estelle throws her arms around him.

This is the kind of attention that makes Jonah cringe with embarrassment, and now that everything's such a mess with Kennedy, I'm not up for this conversation either. "Let's set up over there," I tell Maia and Blake, leaving Jonah to fend for himself.

We reach the top of the hill, and I unfurl the blanket. Bits of dead grass and dirt pop into the sky as the fabric parachutes out and settles onto the lawn. Partway down the hill, Jonah is now wedged between the two stepsisters, trapped in a selfie. His smile says dreamboat, but his eyes say *Help Me.*

I laugh until I realize that Kennedy may see this picture if they post it. Jonah may not be in love with Kennedy right now, but I'm pretty sure she's still into him. How could she not be? How will she feel to see two girls clinging to her man? We've got to bury it on her feed.

I whisper to Maia and Blake, "Selfie." I pull out my phone and flip on the camera, stretching one arm out as far as I can and placing the other on Maia's shoulder. Blake slips a hand on my back and leans his head against mine. His spiky hair tickles my cheek. The jolt sends a panic through me. The church is on fire all over again.

I push the flames down, and in seconds, the photo is posted. I try not to worry that seeing me with Maia might be almost as painful for Kennedy as seeing Jonah with the stepsisters.

Blake settles onto the blanket and breaks out the big bag of popcorn. He taps the seat beside him, but I can't. My stomach is still shaking from the selfie. History has shown what happens when I get like this. Can you imagine if I ruined an entire fireworks show? It's far too dangerous, and there are way too many people around. I pretend I don't see him and wait for Maia to sit beside him. Once she has, I take the place in front of her, as far away from Blake as possible.

He leans forward and taps my shoulder. "Calvin, I actually have something—"

"Sorry about that," Jonah says, having finally

freed himself from the wannabe Kennedy replacements. He takes the one space left, directly in front of Blake. "Hey, we should take a selfie!"

The thought of Blake getting close to me again makes me break into a cold sweat. "Actually, I should probably go to the bathroom." I look to the porta-potties down the lawn that I definitely do not want to go to. Slowly, I rise.

"It'll only take a second." Jonah grabs my pant leg. With his free hand, he pulls out his phone and taps Instagram open. And there on his feed is the photo of Maia, Blake, and me. "Oh," he says. He releases my leg and drops his phone to his side. "Never mind."

"We can definitely take another one," Blake offers helpfully, leaning closer.

"I said I gotta go," I insist, sounding much more frightened than I mean to.

Blake frowns. "Okay."

I force myself to visit a porta-potty. The door clicks closed behind me and I'm greeted by the stink of you-don't-even-want-to-know what. I hold my breath and don't touch anything, standing in the claustrophobic orange plastic space, replaying the brokenhearted "Oh never mind" and "Okay" of my friends over and over again in my mind. After ten or eleven "Oh never mind"s, I push back out into the world and allow myself to breathe.

Nobody says anything when I rejoin the group. Instead we all look down toward the popcorn until it's time to look up at the exploding colors in the sky. Somehow, the booms that shake the ground are less thunderous than our awkward silence.

Sarah drives Blake and me home after the show. I don't comment on the twigs in her hair. I don't say anything at all.

We pull into the driveway. "Well, see ya," I tell Blake as we climb out of the car.

He smirks and extends his hand toward mine. A handshake seems harmless enough, so I reach out. He drops something into my hand. "Have a good night, Calvin," he says, walking away as I roll a small black flash drive around in my palm.

After I've gotten inside and closed my bedroom door behind me, I plug the USB into my laptop. There's a single file titled "Cinderella Edit." Oh boy.

I reluctantly click. If Blake wants me to confront my fears, well, let's see how this goes.

The rainbow wheel spins like an umbrella at the Pride parade until the video player opens, and there I am: shoe in hand, Jonah by my side. So glad we're diving right into this.

"Surely, there must be another eligible foot from whence this shoe came," my friend brilliantly delivers.

I cringe as Film-Me says, "Forsooth," at a perfectly reasonable volume. The image cuts to a closer crop of Kennedy gliding onstage, looking like a serious actress who belongs in New York. My voice continues, "I have foundeth another lady." Wait a second. That isn't how this happened.

The film cuts again, this time to a close-up of a foot sliding into a silver heel. "If you please, sir," Kennedy says. It's not the same shoe, and I'm pretty sure it's not even Kennedy's foot, but my voice on the screen shouts, "Forsooth. It fits!" The audience goes wild with applause as the screen fades to black.

I . . . I don't even know what to say. Blake fixed it. He fixed me.

I pull out my phone. I have to text him, but how can I even express what this means to me? My mind races through my entire vocabulary to find the right words, but all I can see, all I can feel, are fireworks.

KENNEDY

Happy 4th of July!

If you could see what I just saw, you'd see
it wasn't so bad that I fell off the stage.

Actually, sending it now.

Watch this and maybe you can come back?

Did you watch yet?

Seen.

CHAPTER 17

Jonah and I enter the Jewish Assisted Living Center side by side in matching polo shirts and khakis. The lobby smells like the toothpaste they use at the dentist and feels like a giant living room, complete with cozy yellow walls, a beautiful fireplace surrounded by wood paneling, and a dozen or so residents sprinkled around the room.

I practically float to the reception desk beside the door. After Blake's edit, community service doesn't seem so bad after all. Mistakes can be fixed. I can be fixed.

Jonah seems less enthusiastic, still hurt about the selfie incident yesterday. Sarah and Anthony are the least excited of all, still outside parking the car. "We'll be there in a minute," Sarah said as we left them behind in the lot.

A dark-haired woman sitting behind a computer that may be older than some of these residents glances up at us and smiles. A name tag pinned to her chest reads *Nancy*. She looks directly at me and says, "You must be Jonah."

I'm flustered to be confused for such greatness, but maybe the New Me is coming through already.

"No. That's me," he corrects, sounding slightly annoyed. "This is Calvin."

"Oh," Nancy says with a hint of apology. "Well, you'll be working with Charles and Amos." She rises from her seat and leads us over to a pair of guys sitting on either side of a small square table covered in playing cards. Both men must be about eighty years old.

"Amos," the receptionist says, tipping her head toward the man in a wheelchair, who's completely bald and dressed to the nines (or at least the sixes or sevens). "Charles," she says to the man with a full head of wild gray hair who's sporting a dingy plaid bathrobe. "I'd like you to meet Jonah and Calvin."

Amos says, "Nice to meet you, Jonah and Calvin. Have a seat." He gestures to the empty seats around the table, and we settle in across from each other.

Nancy points to a pair of doors behind us.

"Kitchen's that way, bathrooms are down the hall, and I'll be at the desk if you need anything. Have fun, boys." With that, she glides away to the front door, where Sarah and Anthony have finally entered and are waiting for their assignments.

"So," Charles says, "big bar mitzvah coming up, huh?" He's looking at me, the second time somebody has noticed my new confidence and confused me for the Real Star.

"Mine, sir," Jonah says with a shortness that feels out of character.

"Oh, my mistake," says Charles. "Shouldn't have assumed."

I realize I must be missing something. Scanning the room, I register for the first time that most of the staff and all the residents are white.

I glance at Jonah, who shakes his head to stop me from saying anything. I wonder if this is what he meant about not always being able to speak his mind.

"Calvin's Catholic," he tells the guys, "but I sneaked him in."

They laugh. Charles scoops up the deck and starts to shuffle. "You boys know rummy?"

We nod.

"We'll be a team," he says, pointing to himself and Amos, "versus the two of you."

I'm not sure how playing cards is serving the community, but I'm not going to argue.

As Charles deals the cards, Jonah begins to relax, making small talk with the two guys. It's clear that Charles and Amos are close friends, finishing each other's sentences, laughing at each other's jokes, sometimes even before the punch line. It almost feels like Jonah and I are looking at a mirror into our future. I wonder which of us'll be the one with hair.

I reach up to stroke my head, hoping it's me, and spy Sarah across the room listening to a talkative woman who's knitting a blue-and-yellow washcloth. Anthony sits on the armrest of Sarah's chair, his arm draped over her shoulder. So this is why she was so eager to have Anthony join us. I imagine it's hard to find time to spend with your secret boyfriend when your parents monitor your every move.

"I'm out," Amos says as he throws his hand of cards face up onto the table.

Charles cheers. "Are you boys even paying attention?" With effort, he turns his entire torso toward where I've been staring. He nods when he spots

Sarah. With a chuckle, he says, "You can check out that pretty young thing on your own time."

I swear I may vomit right here. "That's my sister!"

"I'm talking about Muriel," he replies. We all laugh.

Jonah clears his throat. "So, how long have you two been . . ." He makes a gesture that encompasses Amos, Charles, and the cards on the table in front of us.

"Gosh," Amos says, "thirty-five years now?"

Wow. No wonder Jonah and I didn't win this game. I've only been playing rummy since my grandma taught me last summer.

Charles nods. "That's right. Few years after my wife died."

"My dad died," Jonah says sympathetically.

"I'm sorry," Charles says.

"Me too," Jonah answers. "But I'm glad you've found happiness again."

"Thanks. It may not always feel like it, but you will too," Charles promises.

We sit in silence for a few moments, until Amos asks, "Say, you boys mind heading into the kitchen and grabbing us some ginger ales?"

"Sure. We'll be right back." Jonah rises and heads toward the kitchen. I follow.

"How cute are they?" I ask as we push open the kitchen doors. The florescent lights click on automatically. We're greeted by sticky red-orange tiles that cover the entire floor and climb halfway up the walls. Assorted pots and pans dangle above the metal island in the middle of the room. One wall is lined with fridges, another with stoves and a sink. Tucked away in the far corner is a soda fountain and a small mountain of stacked plastic glasses.

"Thirty-five years," Jonah says.

"That's so much cards," I say.

"I want that one day." Jonah seems lost in thought, perhaps picturing an elderly version of him and me in a place like this. I wonder if he's imagining me as the one with the hair.

"We'd better start now then," I tease as I pull a glass from the stack and fill it up with ginger ale from the fountain.

"We?"

I don't know if I like cards that much, but he seems excited. "Maybe."

When our eyes meet, Jonah is staring at me with this grin stretched across his face that reminds me of myself pre-show—excited by my pending superstardom and terrified of failure. He's looking at me expectantly, as if there's something else I should be saying.

"Listen, Jonah, about that selfie . . ."

"Don't worry about it," he says. There's silence as I fill a second cup with soda. We turn to the exit and he says softly, "I'm just glad we're hanging out again."

"Me too. And now that Blake's edited the play, everything can go back to normal."

Jonah stiffens. "He edited the play?" We push out of the kitchen and back into the common area.

"He fixed it," I explain.

Jonah grimaces as we pass Sarah, Anthony, and the elderly woman who I swear has an almost full-size blanket draped across her legs now. "He didn't need to do that. You don't need to be fixed, Cal. You're already perfect."

My insides squish.

"This Calvin? Perfect?" eavesdropping Sarah says with a laugh.

"Sarah," Anthony warns my sister, but he's smiling a little too. "Be nice."

Jonah stops and glares at my sister. "Yes. This Calvin. You'd all see that if Kennedy would step out of his spotlight for like one second."

My spotlight? I nearly spill the drink all over Muriel's magically growing blanket. I catch myself in time and keep going toward Charles and Amos.

Kennedy has only been gone for three days, and Jonah has already completely forgotten how things were. How they're supposed to be. Looks like our movie script needs a whole 'nother rewrite.

CHAPTER 18

"Action," Jonah calls out as Blake begins recording. We've tacked some bedsheets to the beams of Jonah's basement ceiling to serve as curtains since we can't get into the school to film on the stage during the summer. Maia stands in the center where Melody belongs, basking in the spotlight of the lamp we've tipped onto its side. Michal and I pose on either side, partially shrouded in shadow.

"What a great rehearsal, Melody," Michal has Kelvin say. For once, Jonah's sister has learned her lines and actually recites them correctly. "Not surprising they gave you the lead in yet another show."

"*Beauty and the Beast* is going to be a blast," I say.

"Hmm?" Melody asks.

"You seem distracted. What are you thinking about?" I ask as Johnny.

"Me? What? Oh, nothing."

"That agent's offer?" Johnny says with a know-ing nod.

Maia bites her lip. "I love it here with you and Kelvin, Johnny, but my dreams are so big and this town is so small."

Something about Maia's tone sounds so authentic that I'm almost reluctant to follow the script and cor-rect her, shaking Johnny's head and *tsk*ing. "There are no small towns, just small actors."

Maia snorts, and I laugh along with her. "That's ridiculous, Calvin."

"Johnny," I correct.

"I'm Calvin," Michal chimes.

"Kelvin," I say.

"Yes?" Jonah's sister asks.

We all laugh again. Even Blake and Jonah are chuckling. The camerawork is going to be shaky, but I saw how Blake cleaned up *Cinderella*, so I am not worried at all.

"Wanna practice our big dance scene, Melody?" I say, continuing with the dialogue I wrote last night.

"Of course, my Beast." Maia holds up her arms and I step forward, taking her left hand in my right and putting my other on her back. Michal steps back since Kelvin has been cast as the Beast's salad fork, who does not appear in the ballroom scene.

Jonah taps his phone and music begins to play.

"You ready?" Maia asks softly, off script.

I nod and begin to count, "One, two, three, one, two, three," with whispered breaths. We spin around the basement, circling Blake with his camera. I stare at Maia/Melody, who grins back at me, having the time of her life. After a while, I start to get dizzy from all the twirling, and Maia blurs into visions of Kennedy in my mind, living her best life in New York.

"I don't want you to leave," I say, tears filling my eyes.

"I know," Maia says, improvising along with me. "But sometimes change can be a good thing. I mean, look at us now." I'm pretty sure she's not talking about Melody and Johnny. "Are we sure her—*me* leaving is a bad thing?"

I stumble, and Maia catches me. "How can you say that?" I suddenly feel very aware of both Jonah and Blake watching—one expecting me to make a mistake he can fix, one convinced I'm perfect. "Look, I know Kelvin could be better," I tell Melody. "But I don't think he's bringing you down. He's—"

"Wait." Maia stops dancing, and I trip again. "Did she really say that to you?"

I feel my face reddening. "Uhhhhhh. Who do you mean, Melody?"

"Calvin."

"Johnny."

"Why are we even doing this?" Maia asks, turning to Blake and Jonah. I keep holding Maia's hand as she steps back, certain that if I let go, the whole world as I know it will slip away forever.

"Okay, pause," Jonah says. "Cut." Our director is probably wishing he never said I was perfect. "Everyone, get in a circle."

We all gather around Jonah, awaiting further orders. "Maia brings up a good question. Why are we doing this?"

I can't believe he's asking. "Because Ken—"

"Shh!" Jonah silences me. "We all know why *you* are doing this, Calvin. But I want to know why everyone else is here."

Maia and Blake both point to me at the same time. Jonah nods. "Same," he says. "But Kennedy means something to me too. My dad thought she was so ridiculous. In a good way." He glances at the boxes of his dad's stuff, packed up in the far corner of the cellar. "At least I think in a good way."

He laughs, and the rest of us grin too.

"The way she could distract us with a song during his treatments. The way she sat with me for hours in silence after we lost him. I'll never forget. I don't know if I want her to stay, but I want her to know."

Maia sighs. "You know, Kennedy's always been kind of everything I wanted to be. She and I never connected the way you guys did, but she knew who I was, we shared a stage, and I did a lot of my best performing as I tried to upstage the princess. She challenged me, and I hate that that means something to me."

"She was the first person to talk to me when I moved here," Blake says. "I was in the hallway, avoiding lunch because, hello, no friends. She asked me if I could take a picture of her because the lighting was *truly spectacular*. Her words. Soon I learned that 'a picture' meant twenty. In every pose imaginable."

Blake mimics some of the trademark poses that the Kennedians eat up. They look even more silly with his fake-tattooed arms.

"She called me a doll, asked for my handle for photo cred, then never spoke to me again until this summer. Was honestly kind of weird, but it was the first time I felt almost welcome in this place. It kind of makes sense I'm back as her behind-the-scenes guy."

Michal clears her throat and shares, "We both like the color pink."

We all cackle at this earth-shattering revelation.

Once he's caught his breath, Jonah looks to Maia. "All right, then. That's why we're doing it."

I smile, and Maia nods.

"Director directing," Blake says, and I think he's not even pretend-impressed this time.

We decide to call it a day after that, so I text Sarah to come get Blake and me. After we've cleaned up a bit, we head toward the stairs.

"Can you hang back for a second, Calvin?" Jonah asks.

"Sure."

When it's just the two of us, I feel the sudden urge to apologize. "I'm sorry you had to do all that. I wrote this scene, and I still couldn't handle it."

Jonah shrugs. "Maybe that's a sign of an exceptional screenwriter."

"Or a pathetic one," I say.

"Stop. You're not pathetic. You just feel things. And I know Kennedy's really going to feel this film. Watching you, I feel things too."

A bead of sweat drips down my forehead.

He adds, "That's a sign of an exceptional actor."

My chest prickles. The greatest actor I've ever known besides Kennedy and the Phantom has given me a compliment I don't deserve, and I can't even describe the feeling. Is it possible for a heart to blush?

"Thanks," I manage. "Was there . . . something you wanted to talk about?"

"Oh, right," Jonah says. "So the other day, at community service . . ." He trails off. I hate that he still doesn't feel like he can tell me everything.

We study each other in silence for a while, and I hope he's remembering those treasured quiet moments with Kennedy.

After a minute, Blake's voice sounds from upstairs: "Calvin, your sister's here!"

"I gotta go. See you later," I tell Jonah. As I run up the stairs, I can't help but remember Kennedy, running away from her Prince at the stroke of midnight.

CHAPTER 19

When I get home, Mom's Bible Study has taken over the living room. All heads turn to greet me: Mrs. Brunelle and Mrs. Buchanan from the sofa, Mom and Mrs. Ruiz from the plush armchairs on the opposite side. A vegetable platter and a plate of crackers rest on the coffee table beside a bowl filled with chopped pinks, reds, and greens—a fancy dip courtesy of Maia's mom, I'm sure.

Mom's guests all say "Hello" at once.

"Good afternoon," I say like the proper gentleman my mother wishes I were.

"Maia told me about the concert," Mrs. Ruiz says, making sure all her friends hear.

"You should have been there," I say, wishing for Maia's sake that she could've been.

"I heard you filmed it. Can I see?"

"Blake has the footage," I tell her. "But it should be in theaters by the end of the summer."

Her mom frowns but nods. We've sold our first ticket!

Suddenly I realize I have another movie that everyone here would love to see. "Actually, let me show you something else."

I turn on the TV and connect my phone. A minute later, Blake's edit of *Cinderella* is streaming in our living room. It's even more glorious on the big screen, and when it finishes, Mom's friends clap.

Mom seems genuinely proud. "That was lovely, Calvin. How did you do this?"

"Blake did it."

The silence that falls over the room speaks for everyone's dislike of a kid they've never met.

"Well," Mrs. Brunelle cautiously says, "he did a great job."

Everyone seems to relax and agree.

I excuse myself to my room and scroll through Kennedy's Instagram until dinner. It's been six days since she left, but she's only texted once. It's almost like she's forgotten about me, though I Like every post I've missed. Unpacking suitcases in her mother's apartment. Visiting Times Square. Standing beneath the *Hamilton* marquee. I flip to my texts and open my conversation with her, but I don't even know what else to say.

After dinner, I find myself back on her page, wedged between my parents on the sofa. Their noses are also glued to their phones, while the local news plays on the TV, unwatched. Kennedy has already shared two new posts since dinner. In the latest, she stands on a stage I don't recognize with her arm thrown around some blond girl I don't know. *Practicing for the summer showcase. Already love NYYAPA and my new BFF.*

Your what?! I can't decide which is worse: Kennedy having a new BFF or starring in a show without me.

Mom looks up at me. "The girls loved that film you shared, Calvin. Maia's mom really can't wait to see what you can do with the July Fourth footage."

"What Blake does," I correct.

Mom grimaces.

"Film?" Dad asks.

"His 'friend' fixed *Cinderella*." The air quotes surrounding the word *friend* are not lost on me.

"Maybe he's not so bad after all," Dad says, sounding impressed.

I cannot believe Dad actually said that. "He's not," I say. "The tattoos aren't real, by the way. Plus they're mostly chickens and things." Dad laughs, though it's clear that Mom is not amused.

I hate to see them disagreeing yet again because of me. How much strain can one kid put on a marriage before it snaps? The barbecue chicken we had for dinner lurches in my stomach. I clench and shrink deeper into the sofa, muttering, "I'm sorry."

"For what?" Mom asks.

They're both looking at me, waiting for me to respond, and I don't think "Forsooth" will cut it. I take a breath and realize I have so much to be sorry about. I haven't been their favorite child lately, and since their only other kid is Sarah, that's saying something. "About embarrassing you. At the church. And in the show. And always."

Mom reaches out and grabs my knee. She squeezes. "We know, honey."

She's smiling as best she can, but her tired eyes are still sad.

"I'm such a disappointment."

"Calvin." Dad looks even more exhausted. "You are not," he lies.

"Sure, Dad," I say as if I believe him.

I'm really doing a number on them, aren't I? I wish I could make them happy for one second instead of letting them down again and again and again. Maybe if I can help them remember a time they were truly happy together, they'll stop disagreeing about everything. Unfortunately, I've made so many messes lately, I'm going to have to go way back.

Looking from one parent to the other, I ask, "Can I see your wedding pictures?"

Mom's spine straightens and her eyes light up. She hops to her feet as though she's been waiting for this moment all her life. As she dashes across the room to a drawer in our TV stand, Dad puts down his phone. He doesn't say anything, but as Mom pulls out a flat, flowery box and rests it on the coffee table, he leans forward.

She kneels and raises the lid slowly. It seems heavy, airtight, as if the box hasn't been opened in years. It makes a little fart sound that I struggle not to laugh at. I scoot to my knees for a front row seat. With the lid aside, I see the square cutout on the black leather cover, a peekaboo to page one showing my parents with their arms around each other, twenty years younger. Mom looks like Sarah, and

Dad looks, well, happy. I open the book, revealing the full picture. It's beautiful. My fingers swipe over the protective plastic as if I can feel the lace in a photo.

Dad scoots off the couch and kneels beside me. "Fingerprints," he warns, but I know he's not really mad.

Mom slowly flips through the pages. "Who's that?" I ask every time somebody new appears.

"Your aunt Helen." "My best friend from college." "Your dad's roommate." "Our old neighbors." "I have no idea."

When we find their first dance, Mom pauses, taking in some long-ago memory. Dad's arm brushes my back as he reaches across. He rests a hand on Mom's lower back and begins to hum.

Mom begins to sway, bumping into my side so I fall into my dad's armpit. Who knew my scheme would work so quickly? I think they're about to get a little intimate, which is not what I signed up for, but I don't know how to escape when I'm trapped between my parents and a coffee table, and I haven't seen them act like this in, um, ever, so who am I to destroy their one moment of happiness in months, but who are they to do this in front of me?

I close my eyes and take a breath like Blake showed me, because if I panic here I could destroy a marriage. Mercifully, Dad's arm drops to his side again, and Mom closes the book.

We sit in silence for a few moments, filling in all the memories of everything that's happened since that last picture. When Sarah and I were born. When I fell off the stage. When I almost us got us kicked out of church because Blake made me feel . . . I try to shake the thought from my mind, and I must actually shake my head, because Mom and Dad both shift to face me.

"What's going on, kiddo?" Dad asks.

"Nothing," I say too quickly. "I've got to go to bed." I push myself up and try my best to look like I'm not running away. "Thanks for showing me the photos. Night."

Out in the hallway, where they can't see me, I freeze to eavesdrop.

Mom whispers with a chuckle. "I think we scared him."

"Maybe he's starting to have some feelings of his own."

"Kennedy?" There's pity in her voice.

"He'll find someone else."

And that's enough for me. I retreat to my bedroom and close the door behind me. First of all, I don't need someone *else* because Kennedy is not the one for me. And second of all, there is no one for me anyway because I am thirteen and I am such a mess and why would anybody want anything to do with me?

As if on cue, there is a knock on my window.

CHAPTER 20

Blake stands beside my bed, waiting for me to tell him what Jonah wanted earlier. I'm certain my parents will barge in here any minute and send me to confession faster than they can say, *What the heck is Blake doing in your room?*

"Jonah wanted to say he likes my script," I finally whisper once it seems that the coast is clear.

"Really?" Blake sounds surprised, which only hurts a little.

"And something about feelings."

"Oh?"

"He never finished his thought." I shrug. It's becoming a habit with Jonah lately. "Probably distracted by bar mitzvah stuff."

Blake frowns. I know Jonah sent the invitations out months ago, but I really thought he would've given Blake a last-minute invite by now considering how much we've all been hanging out this summer. I swear I saw him pass one to Maia the other day when he thought we weren't looking.

"Anyway," Blake says, "do you have any plans tonight?"

"Oh, yeah. Big plans, you know me." I laugh because I have never had plans after 7 p.m., other than Brush My Teeth, Get Into Bed, and Consider Texting Kennedy after Social Media Stalking Her for a Couple of Hours. "Thinking I'd catch an evening show at the theater and close out the night at the club."

I wait for Blake to laugh along, but his lips and eyebrows sink farther down. "My parents are having . . . a moment, and I need a distraction. Maybe I can come with?"

"Blake, I'm not really—"

"I know," he says. "But maybe we could pretend?"

I smile. "You mean acting." Now he's speaking my language.

"Kind of," he says, reaching behind me to grab a pillow. I study the armadillo in a bowler hat drawn on his arm in blue pen as he stuffs the pillow under my blanket and tucks it in, making it almost look like someone is beneath the covers. "Acting like you're here."

He wants me to sneak out? For the first time, I wonder if Mom and her friends might be right about him.

We're face to face. His storm-cloud eyes beg me to join him. My stomach drops like the chandelier in *The Phantom of the Opera* as I imagine Blake's hand on my back, his face inches from mine. I shake the thought from my mind. Why would it even go there? I think I'm blushing. I can't even look Blake in the eye as I struggle to catch my breath.

He notices, tilting his head down so our eyes meet again. "What do you say?"

I say nothing.

"My dad is afraid of everything too, Calvin," he says. "And I sometimes wonder, if he took some chances, tried something fun . . ."

My stomach turns. Fun like climbing out the window and doing something without my parents' permission? That sounds like a very bad idea.

But Blake is a fixer. Plus, he has a therapist. What could possibly go wrong?

I study my friend. He's wearing dark skinny jeans and I catch a hint of grown-up cologne. It almost feels like this was his plan all along. "I don't smell good enough to go out," I protest.

He leans in and brings his nose inches from my cheek. I guess I'm finally growing some of that much-desired facial hair, because it sticks straight up as he inhales. Goose bumps cover my arm as I picture turning my neck to bump noses with Blake. What is wrong with me?

"You smell fine," Blake says. "Trust me."

He knows he's got me. How can I not trust the person who has helped me feel less afraid all summer? "Okay, let's do it."

"Lock your door and turn out the lights to be safe," he instructs, so I do.

With that, Blake slides out the window. I throw one leg out, followed by the other, and sit on the sill waiting a moment for something to stop me. Nothing happens. No Dad yelling or God flashing a bolt of lightning. I slide out, the siding of our house scraping my back on the way down. With a *thunk*, I land on my butt, crushing the plants beneath. Blake holds out a helping hand, and I take it. He hoists me up with a grunt. Who knows how I'll get back in later, but that problem is a whole adventure away.

Blake reaches around and swishes the debris

from my butt. My cheeks clench. The next thing I know, he's grabbing my hand and saying, "Let's go," so we go.

I am so afraid of everything and everyone that I don't let go of his hand for the entire twenty-five-minute walk to Main Street, the only place in town that's awake at this time. We don't say much, but occasionally when my heart gets especially thumpity, his thumb strokes my knuckles, and I know we're okay.

As a car whizzes by, I finally pull my hand away, planting it safely in my pocket. I don't want anyone getting the wrong idea, and I especially don't want that wrong idea finding its way back to my parents.

"We're almost there," Blake says. We pass the 7-Eleven and the hardware store and Belladonna's, the vintage clothing store where Kennedy shops when trying to really get into a role.

Finally, we duck into an alley that is not at all sketchy. By that, I mean I've seen enough movies to know I'm going to have to pass on this one. Sorry, Blake. Two dumpsters line a chain-link fence in the back, and I swear I can hear a dozen rats scurrying in the shadows. I slam on the brakes.

"Trust me," Blake says. In spite of myself, I do. Halfway along the dirty brick wall, there's an unmarked door flanked by three vintage movie posters on either side. A light bulb flickers above each poster, creating an eerie buzz.

Blake stops in front of one of the posters. It looks like a Batman comic book, with bright yellow text popping off the mysterious red-caped figure. I take in the words across the top: *The Phantom of the Opera*.

"What?" I exclaim.

He smiles. "Thought you'd appreciate seeing the original film. It's from the 1920s! Plus, maybe it'll help with the love story bit of our movie. I don't really believe the Jonah character loves Melody."

"Johnny," I correct.

"Right," Blake says. "But they're totally a thing, right?" It's only a question, but somehow it doesn't feel like we are talking about our movie at all.

"Yes," I promise.

He gives me a "Right on" sort of nod and bumps my shoulder, nudging me into the dimly lit theater that I never knew was here and that still kinda scares me.

My nostrils are greeted by the scent of popcorn, and I feel a little better. Blake pulls out a twenty and hands it to the ticket seller. "Two for *Phantom* and a small popcorn."

"Aw, hey, Blake!" the cashier says. I glance up and all excitement flees my body, replaced by sheer terror.

"Calvin?" says my sister's boyfriend, Anthony. He's wearing a greasy red-and-white striped shirt and a stunned expression.

Blake notices my pale face, which must resemble the Phantom's. As he hands Anthony the money, he says, "You can keep a secret, right? We snuck out."

Anthony seals his lips with an imaginary zipper.

I'm not fully confident that he can resist telling my sister the scandal of the century. Even if he could, I frantically try to calculate how long it will take to see a whole movie *and* walk home, plus the time it's already taken to walk here. Whether Anthony snitches or not, it'll be a miracle if Mom and Dad don't notice I'm gone before I'm back. This is a complete disaster.

"Breathe, Calvin," Blake whispers for the zillionth time since I've met him, and somehow, it helps.

I look at Blake, aiming his crooked smile at Anthony as he drops his extra change in the tip cup, and I melt like the butter Anthony drizzles over our popcorn. I send up a quick prayer to my pal God, asking for a teensy miracle, because there's no way I'm going anywhere besides into that theater with this boy.

The movie is so terrifying that I accidentally grab Blake's hand no fewer than three times. The last time, he locks his pinky around mine, and we stay this way until the lights come on.

On the walk home, my mind goes a million places, and I babble them all to Blake—"How awesome was that?" "I've never seen a silent movie before." "Do you think my parents'll know I've sneaked out?" "Do you think Anthony told on us?" "How dead am I?" The only question I don't wonder out loud is whether his pinky is still burning too.

KENNEDY

?!?!?!?!

Seen.

CHAPTER 21

In honor of my parents not busting me last night, I decide not to set the church on fire for our second choir performance. It doesn't hurt that Ms. Clarkson puts Maia and me in the very back row, even though we're too short to be seen by anyone from here. This is a good thing because I lost the only adult choir robe that almost fit me, so she's given me a bright blue kid's robe, and I stand out like a peacock at a penguin party.

"You look terrible," Maia whispers to me.

"I should not have thrown away that robe," I agree.

"No, I mean you look exhausted."

"I was out late last night," I quietly explain, before mentally smacking myself in the head. What am I doing? I glance up at the statue of Jesus to see if He's heard.

"Doing what?"

I definitely shouldn't tell her the truth, but friends don't lie to each other, right? (Summer solo excluded.)

"I sneaked out," I whisper.

"You? Calvin Conroy?" She almost forgets to use her hushed, church-gossip voice.

"You can call me Bad Sandy," I say, picturing myself at the end of *Grease* with leather pants and a fake cigarette. My fingers form a V, bringing the imaginary cigarette to my lips. I exhale slowly but after a moment force out a cough because even pretending to smoke is gross.

Maia laughs out loud. "You have to tell me about it later."

I'm not sure if I can even put it into words. Blake and I stared at each other for like thirty seconds outside my window last night while my feet shuffled around in the grass. Finally, I leaned in and gave him a handshake-hug before softly saying, "This was *Phan*tastic." He chuckled, then helped to hoist me up the side of the house into my darkened bedroom. The door hadn't been broken down, and the hallway was quiet. My parents hadn't noticed anything. I was filled with relief as I watched Blake race across the backyard toward his own house, accompanied by the sound of squishing grass and my whirring heart.

Now I glance again at Jesus, who says nothing.

Beneath Him, Father Paul approaches the pulpit in a crisp new robe. He starts his homily, also known as the part where I can have a little me time and zone out. I'm about to reprocess everything that happened yesterday when there's an unsettling murmur in the church. My eyes refocus and I swear it seems that all the heads in the room are slowly turning to look at me.

Like the parting of the Red Sea, the two kids in front of me bend in either direction so the congregation has an unobstructed view of me, bright blue kiddie robe and all. I glance over my shoulder, wondering if there's something behind me that we're all looking at, but the only thing there is a brick wall. I hear a few scattered chuckles. My face flushes turquoise beneath the stained glass.

I glance to Father Paul, whose gaze is locked on me. "Come on up here, Calvin," he says warmly, and I wonder what in the world I missed in that twenty-second daydream.

I squeeze my fists and will myself to melt into

the floor, but when that doesn't work, I rise to my feet. I'm not about to let my moment in the spotlight be in a baby robe, though, so I quickly wriggle it over my head and toss it behind me before pushing through the choir. My eyes flicker from candle to candle. There's only like three in the whole church, but with everyone staring at me, waiting, and some even hoping (Sarah!) for me to burn the place down, I keep my steps slow and steady. I glimpse Mom squirming in the front row, Dad looking downright angry, and Sarah loving this moment.

When I finally reach the little podium thingy, Father Paul's hand clenches down on my shoulder as he spins me around to face the crowd. "This young man," he declares with the kind of chuckle you use when you know you're being hilarious, "really sparked my homily." The whole room fills with the sound of polite laughter. I'm instantly brought back to the school theater, silver slipper in hand.

I peer toward the back of the church, wondering if it's possible to make a break for the exit. Way in the last pew I see . . . My mouth drops open. Jonah? He nods, and suddenly all this, whatever this is, seems almost okay.

"I literally ripped my clothes off in front of all

of you," Father Paul jokes. More laughter. I also just ripped my robe off in front of everyone, so if we could wrap this torture up, I'd like to know what Jonah's doing here.

Father Paul continues, "I could've gotten embarrassed. Or mad. I could've kicked this boy and his poor parents out of the parish."

Oh, no. Mom fidgets as the scowl across Dad's face deepens. I hope they lathered up on the deodorant today because I can tell they're just as mortified as I am. I have to stop this. "You can't," I protest.

Father Paul guffaws. "Oh, can't I?" he says, a playful challenge.

I take a deep breath and try to ignore the rest of the crowd. "You can kick *me* out of church, because I'm the one who messed up, and maybe even Sarah, because she's graduating next year anyway, but my parents really like it here."

The sculpted Jesus's mouth is twisted in concern.

I gulp again. "Not that I don't like it here too, but I'm young, you know, and I'll be okay, your highness. Holiness. Sir." I flick my fingers into a quick sign of the cross.

Everyone laughs. Even Father Paul is grinning. "It's okay, kiddo. Man, you're killin' 'em today."

He finally releases me and gestures to the crowd. "I should really have you up here every week. Maybe we could even go on tour."

Am I actually doing okay up here? I consider the comedy stylings of Calvin and Father Paul On Tour. Well, that's certainly one way to stardom. Can you picture Kennedy's face if I manage to join a sellout international tour before her?

"Okay, I'll do it!" I exclaim.

Father Paul's brow furrows. "Do what?"

Shoot. I've interrupted the actual valuable lesson. I cover as best I can. "I will, uh, keep doing the community service you assigned me as punishment for ruining your robe."

There's an awkward silence. Father Paul looks flustered. I think I've gone off message.

"Ah, that," he says, choosing his next words carefully. "Yes, well, of course I forgave this young man, as I was saying, but I've also instilled in him a sense of duty and community. Now tell me, Cal, what have you decided to do to serve your community?"

"I'm helping at the Jewish Assisted Living Center. I play cards with old men and my friend Jonah. It's a hoot." I smile toward Jonah in the back.

"Forgiveness, everyone," Father Paul says, gently pushing me forward, my cue to exit stage left. "Learn it. Live it. Love it."

The crowd loves us. I wave to the audience and return to the rear of the choir.

Dad tries to stop me at the end of the service, but I push past him to get to Jonah, who's waiting for me by the exit. "Are you converting?"

He snorts. "Oh yeah. Bar mitzvah practice was getting to be a lot. Thought this'd be easier, but man, was it painful watching you up there."

"I thought I killed it. But you know, I don't think this comedy tour thing is gonna work out after all. He kind of bombed at the end, didn't he?"

Jonah nods. "I wouldn't book the tour bus yet." He throws a hand up onto my shoulder. Second time within the hour someone has been clinging to that very shoulder, but this time, it feels nice.

"Really, though," I ask, "what are you doing here?"

He flashes that gap-toothed grin that drives the seventh-grade drama maidens wild. "I didn't want you to have to run as far. You know. If something went wrong."

My insides smoosh. This is the kindest thing he's done for me in forever. I playfully bump my shoulder against his and hope he understands.

CHAPTER 22

I can tell my parents want *so badly* to punish me when we get home, but it's not my fault that the priest embarrassing me embarrassed them, so instead the General mumbles something about being respectful, and Mom gives me permission to go to Maia's after lunch.

Maia's got the most vibrant bedroom I've ever seen. Hangers holding some of her best costumes from the school shows are tacked to the walls, popping against painted stripes of turquoise, orange, and green. Once I settle in, Maia wants to hear the dirt on my date, and . . .

Sorry, not date. Friend outing.

Wait. Not outing like Outing.

"Wow," she says when I've finished telling her everything, except the pinkies and the feelings and the truth about the solo. "I'm jealous. I've never been on a date before."

"It wasn't a date," I insist, glancing toward the doorway to make sure her mother isn't lurking in the hall. I never should've said anything. "Can we just work on your song?"

"You sure there's nothing else? Because, you know, if you want to talk about anything, I'm here."

I shrug. "Thanks. I'm good, though."

"I'm glad we're friends now," she says abruptly. "You and Jonah always used to hang with Kennedy. I didn't mind when Nika still lived here, but after she moved away . . . I don't know, I felt like I belonged in your group but wasn't allowed in. Now I'm here, and it makes sense, you know?"

I never thought about it like that, but it does feel kind of right.

"My mom loves helping with the school shows—the costumes and stuff—but I feel like my parents don't think I'm doing anything important. Now, my brothers with their soccer, that's gonna lead to something, they're so sure. But my dreams . . ." She trails off and looks at the costumes hanging on her wall. "They're a hobby to squeeze in around your real work. This solo will finally show them my dreams matter, too." She pauses, giving the guilt a moment to nestle into my chest. "It means a lot to me. So, if there's ever anything you want to talk about, and I mean, *anything* . . ."

It's a very pointed Anything that I can tell means Everything, which makes me feel like a big lying Nothing.

"Thanks," I tell her. "I'll, uh, keep that in mind." We spend the rest of the afternoon selecting a song for Maia's audition, plus some other songs for Kennedy's film.

When I get home, Mom stops me in the hallway. "Put on some nice clothes. You have a date."

"A what?" The floor drops out beneath me as I remember my not-a-date from last night.

But as it turns out, by *date*, Mom was actually using the most embarrassing wording possible to describe some awkward one-on-one time with my dad. He wants to take me to Sal's for pizza, "just us guys."

One hour later, a muted TV tacked onto the wall behind me illuminates the pizza parlor. We're supposed to be bonding, but the General keeps glancing at the soccer players racing across the screen. I don't even think he likes soccer, but at least it's more interesting than me.

"Listen, Calvin," he finally says, his eyes darting down for a moment. There must be a commercial. "I wanted to talk about yesterday. The things you were saying . . . I guess I was wondering. Are you okay?" It almost sounds like he cares.

"Yeah, sorry. I guess I've had a lot on my mind lately."

"Like what?" he asks, and seriously, since when has my dad taken such an interest in my thoughts?

My pinkie twitches, intertwining with Blake's in my memory. It's almost like he knows. That theater wasn't that crowded last night, and I don't think I saw anyone from church there. Besides, as I told Maia: Blake is my friend. He is fixing me. There is nothing else to know.

"Church," I lie.

"You did well today," Dad says with a smile. It's almost comforting to know we're both liars.

Our server, Gio, sets a steaming tray between my dad and me. "Half peppers and onions, half pepperoni. Can I get you anything else?"

I lift my glass. The ice slushes as I shake it around. "Can I have another soda, please?"

"Ab. So. Loot. Ly." Gio says like some kind of ecstatic robot. He snatches the glass from me and bounces away.

Dad serves us each a slice. The melty, oozy cheese is exactly what we need to end our conversation and move on to the part of the evening where our mouths are too full to talk, followed by the part where I go home and text Maia that she misinterpreted what happened with Blake—

"See. That!" Dad's pointing to my face. I haven't even taken a bite yet, so how can I have sauce on my chin already? "With a big old grin like that, don't tell me you're not thinking of something." There's a moment of silence before he leans in and adds a mortifying, "Or someone." I can practically see the pair of winking emojis in his tone, a tone he has never used with me before. A tone I cannot trust, even if I want to when he says, "Talk to me, Cal."

I'm super grateful Sal's is so poorly lit now so Dad doesn't see the hairs on my neck shooting straight up or the terror creeping into my eyes. I hadn't even realized I'd been smiling.

"Is it Maia?"

I can't think about Maia without remembering what she suggested today, and I can't remember what she suggested without remembering that I am the General's worst nightmare.

"Dad. Stop. It's not Maia. It's not anyone." I throw out the grouchiest "Please leave me alone" that I can.

Out of nowhere, a hand reaches down in front of me, and I scream. Gio nearly spills my orange soda all over me. He saves it just in time. Everyone in the restaurant stops to stare, which I'm sure is tearing Dad apart.

"I am so sorry, sport," Gio says, bringing his hand to his heart.

He has the terrified look of someone about to lose his job, but Dad reassures him. "He's fine. You're fine." His eyes lock with mine as he firmly says, "Everything's fine." The no-nonsense tone is back because I've embarrassed him again.

Gio walks away, but everyone else is stealthily keeping their attention on us. If they know anything about me, they know it's only a matter of time before I knock over the table or accidentally commit arson. Still, nothing can compare to the devastated eyes of my father, who tried to be friendly for once in his life before I bit his head off.

"I'm sorry, Dad," I whisper. "It's just . . ." For one second, I consider telling him everything. One Mississippi. When the second passes, I bite my lip and say, "The pizza's getting cold."

He watches me take an enormous bite. "You know that God has a plan for us all, right, Cal?"

I don't know if my face is burning from the question or from the bite of pizza that is not as cold as I said. My tongue is on fire, but spitting my food out would mean embarrassing Dad more than I already have.

I finally swallow the scorching glob of cheese and take a swig of my drink. "I know what God thinks."

"He thinks you're great, Cal. And He wants you to trust me." His tone is soft and kind again. Who is this man, what has he done with the General, and why do I almost believe him?

Dad finally picks up his own slice of pizza. His eyes lock on the TV as he chews, and I try to digest what is happening.

I'm grateful that God's plan doesn't come up again during the rest of the meal or the ride home, but I can't pull my mind from my dad nearly begging me to trust him.

We're still ten minutes from home when he parks the car in front of the 7-Eleven and opens the door. "Come on. I've got a surprise for you," he says as he slides out and closes the door behind him.

We walk down the sidewalk a while until we reach a familiar sketchy alley that I wouldn't be caught dead walking down . . . two nights in a row.

"What are we doing here?" I'm unable to hide my alarm as Dad turns toward the hidden movie theater. We stop in front of the *Phantom* poster. Does he know I was here with Blake last night? Is this a trap to make me confess? God has a plan. Is this it? My armpits moisten.

Dad's soft, freezing-cold fingers wrap around the back of my neck. I shudder. "I know it's not the musical, but I used to love this kind of movie as a kid. If nothing else, I think some of my favorite ball players are in it." He snorts at his own reference to the posters in my bedroom that I decorated with *Phantom* masks.

With his fingers still clinging to my neck, he guides me inside the theater.

"Calvin!" There's Anthony in the same greasy

striped shirt. I wonder if he's even washed it. "Back so soon?"

I shoot Anthony some murder eyes and tip my head toward my dad.

"Sorry," he says apologetically. "I meant, uh, it feels like it was just this morning I saw you at the pulpit during the homily. Great stuff."

"Anthony's from church," I explain to my dad. It feels cold, but it's what Sarah would want.

"Ah," Dad nods. "You Barry's kid?"

It's Anthony's turn to blush. "Yes, sir. Nice to meet you, sir." I think he's shaking, and I wonder how hard it must be to meet your girlfriend's father when he doesn't know you even exist. Anthony extends a hand that is as buttery as the stains on his shirt.

Dad looks at the hand, then holds up two fingers. "Two to *Phantom*, please."

"Yes, sir. Of course, sir." Anthony's nervousness almost matches mine.

We exchange a sympathetic smile before Dad collects the tickets and leads me into the theater.

This time, the movie is truly agonizing. I jump at all the same moments, but Blake isn't there to clutch my pinky. Wishing that he was makes me all the guiltier. When the movie ends and Dad beams down at me, it's clear he doesn't know the truth. My father was really being nice, thinking of me in a way that I didn't even realize he could, and somehow, that makes me feel even worse.

CHAPTER 23

I wait for Blake to call or text or show up at my window, but he doesn't. In fact, he doesn't call the next day either. I try not to let Jonah know I'm concerned during community service, but his eyebrows arch and my face reddens when Anthony asks if Blake and I enjoyed the movie.

I change the subject as quickly as I can before Sarah can overhear.

I ask my sister to drop me off at Blake's house on the way home. As I approach the front door, I realize I've never been to his house before. I press the doorbell and wait. After a good twenty seconds, I press the button again. I can hear the chimes bouncing around inside.

Finally, the doorknob rattles and the door creaks open.

A pale man with dark shoulder-length hair peeks through the crack. He flashes a smile without teeth, and I can't tell if he's happy or afraid to see me.

"Hi," I say.

He nods. "Hello."

"Is Blake here?"

"Yes."

I wait for him to go get his son, but when he doesn't move, I ask, "Can I see him?"

"I'm sorry." He takes a deep slow breath, in and out, and I can almost hear Blake whisper, *Breathe, Dad, breathe.* "Are you Calvin?"

"Yes, sir." I nod, my face prickling as I think of all the reasons Blake might be home but unable to see me. Sleeping. Mad. Sick. Doesn't like me. Dead.

"He's grounded. You wouldn't know anything about him sneaking out, would you?"

Blake got caught?! I hope his dad interprets my stunned expression and silence as wide-eyed innocence.

His crystal-blue eyes scan me with a gaze that doesn't seem fooled at all.

"Please don't tell my parents," I beg. I feel so guilty. I've let the General down and violated all three Rs: rejected the Rules, ruined my Reputation, and refused Responsibility. Even worse, I've gotten Blake in trouble.

"That's between you and them," Blake's dad says, and I fill with a fourth R, relief. "But I have enough to worry about, Calvin," he warns as though it was my idea to sneak out.

Blake's dad starts to close the door.

"Can I ask you a question?" I say in a rush.

He pauses and tips his head ever so slightly, which I take as a yes.

"Blake says you're a lot like me. And I guess I'm just wondering: Does it ever get quieter, like inside your head?"

"For some people," he says, not very convincingly. He must see the horror across my face as he adds, "It will for you." A flash of Blake's reassurance creeps into his smile.

I smile back and promise my days of sneakery are over.

"I really am glad he's found a friend. Blake will see you in a week," his dad promises, closing the door.

As I tramp across the lawn, I text Maia and Jonah: Blake's grounded. No filming today.

Jonah replies instantly: Can you still come over?

Sure. See you soon.

When I get to his house, Jonah takes me directly into the basement.

"Kinda nice that we can have some more time alone," he admits, and honestly, it's kind of nice to hear him say it.

"Yeah," I agree. "Stinks about Blake, though."

"Not our fault." It sounds more like a question. He's probably waiting for me to explain what Anthony said at community service, but that secret stays with Blake, Blake's dad, Anthony, and me.

"Soooo what do you feel like doing?" I ask. "Since we can't film?"

"Well, I was hoping you could brainstorm with me," Jonah says. "I've been thinking about my dad. I want to honor him. At my bar mitzvah, you know? But I haven't figured out how yet."

I glance toward the boxes of his dad's stuff stacked in the corner. "Maybe there's something in there?"

We wander over toward the boxes and each open one. I pull out a dark blue necktie. "Could you wear this?" I ask, throwing it over his shoulder.

"That's perfect." He pauses and pulls the framed photo of his family out of his box. He rubs his finger over the glass. "She'd never say it, but I think it's gonna be hard for Mom to go through it without him."

"Can you honor her too?" I ask.

"What do you mean?"

I try to think of what might make my parents happy. "May I?" I ask, before digging into his box and pulling out the wedding album I recall seeing a few weeks ago.

I flip it open. We both gaze at the photo. His parents are dancing—his mom with an Afro, his dad in a slick chocolate tux.

Jonah's quiet for a few moments as we study the picture. They both look so happy. My folks loved their trip down memory lane. Would Jonah's mom, or would it be a painful reminder of what she's lost?

"Could you frame it?" I ask.

He shakes his head, takes the book from me, and gently places it back in the box. "Maybe I could dance with my mom to their song."

He pulls out his phone and begins to play a song. A nice mellow beat fills the space.

"And maybe you could help me practice." He spins to face me, taking my right hand in his left. *Friends hold friends' hands all the time*, I remind myself. His cold palms send a chill down my spine. His right hand reaches out and creeps around my hip, pulling me closer to him. Our chests are almost touching.

I feel butterflies as he leads me around the basement.

I know I should pull away because he is Kennedy's one true love even if their first kiss came too soon. Blake's pointed question from our date—sorry, not a date—chimes in my head: *Melody and Johnny are totally a thing, right?*

Of course, I reassure myself, because what would my parents say if anything else were true, and what if Michal comes down, and why does that matter since we're just two friends practicing for a very special performance, and can he hear my heart beating right now?

I try to focus on the vocals coming from Jonah's phone. The singer croons about how no matter what happens, she'd never leave your side, baby.

"Is this song about us?" I ask.

"Huh?"

"I thought you were pushing me away. You promised me you weren't."

Jonah laughs. "Uh, this is my parents' wedding song. It's called 'By Your Side.' By someone named Sade."

I nod, feeling more than a little embarrassed. Why would he dance to a song about me with his mother to honor his father?

"It's cute, though," Jonah whispers, his breath flipping the hair above my ear and sending a prickle down my spine, "that it reminds you of us."

I swear his grip on my hip pulls me in a little closer. My whole body stiffens as he glides me across the floor.

One two three. One two three. One two three. Run shoo flee.

I should pull away, but Jonah starts singing along to the track, and he has the nicest voice I've ever heard (besides Kennedy's and Maia's, of course). We both know I'm not going anywhere. I do my best to channel Kennedy—the one who belongs here with him—by leaning my head on his shoulder like I'm his girlfriend at the eighth-grade semiformal, feeling like a cross between my parents' worst nightmare and a sloppy puddle on the floor.

"One two three one two three one two three." As Jonah leads me around the room, slowly the fears fade from my mind, and it's just him and me and the whole world spinning and spinning and smiling and spinning.

KENNEDY

Hey. Me again. I don't know if you're getting these messages, but I could really use a friend right now, and I don't know who else to talk to.

Maia says I can tell her anything, but she's perfectly fine with certain things that I really can't be. Anyway, you know when the Phantom gets in the way of Christine and Raoul's true love? I think that's me. The Phantom. The actor who played him in Phantom 2 said I was going to be him one day, but I don't think this is what he had in mind. And it's not what I had in mind either. I told Maia I'm fine, but I'm not so sure. I sneaked out of the house to see a movie one night and for a second I thought things were <3 Things <3 with somebody even though I know they can't be, but then today I was dancing with someone else and totally thought

things were <3 Things <3 with Jonah,
but like, What even? My parents would
kill me. The scandal of it all. I really
wish I had somebody to talk to.

Crap. That second things
were <3 Things <3 should say
"with that someone else"

Not Jonah.

Sorry. That was a typo.

Ignore me please.

I am so, so sorry.

Seen.

CHAPTER 24

Kennedy doesn't respond to any of my messages. I even try to call her once and she sends me to voicemail. I have no choice but to read between the lines of every one of her social media posts. I navigate to her page and find the warning, *KenSeeMeInLights has blocked you.*

"What?!" The panicked string of words that flies through my mind would bring my mother to her knees in prayer. Blocked? Because of a misunderstanding?

Sarah pokes her head into my room. "You okay?" she asks as if she cares.

"Kennedy blocked me!" The words sound even more vile than any word on Mom's forbidden list. "Can I borrow your phone? I need to see her page."

Sarah shakes her head. "Calvin, friendships aren't supposed to be this hard."

"Mom's are," I say. I've never seen somebody struggle so hard to keep a group of people happy. "And mine aren't any easier."

"Seems like it was pretty easy slipping out with Blake the other night."

My jaw drops to the floor. "Anthony told you?"

"Bold move taking Dad on the same date the next night." She snorts.

"Obviously I didn't plan that." Dad and I haven't spoken much since he took me to the movies, and this reminder of guilt is the last thing I need right now.

Her tone softens as she asks, "What really happened between you and Kennedy?"

I don't know how to tell her what happened without telling her what happened between me and Jonah.

Sarah stands in my doorway for a minute, waiting for me to say something, anything, but I can't. "Well, you know where to find me," she says, patting the door jamb twice.

Alone again, I glare at my phone. Without access to Kennedy, it feels broken, disconnected, just like my friendship. This movie with my friends isn't going to convince Kennedy to stay because of me. It needs to convince her to stay *in spite of* me.

I spend the rest of the week locked up in my room revising the last two scenes of the script. This new arc will prove to my friends exactly how not-in-the-way of the love story of the century I am. (*The Phantom of the Opera* wasn't this century, right?)

A week later, Maia, Michal, Jonah, Blake, and I all gather in Jonah's basement. "Check your emails," I say.

They all pull out their phones. "What's this?" Jonah asks.

"Rewrite."

"Again?" Maia moans.

"Do you know how many times Andrew Lloyd Webber had to rewrite *Phantom 2* before it became the phenomenon we saw last month?"

"No."

I was really hoping somebody would chime in with a theater fun fact here, but Jonah, Blake, and Michal don't seem to know either. "At least twice," I finally state.

"I'm game for anything," Blake says, supposedly talking about the script, but I can't help thinking about the movie excursion that got him punished for a whole week. The Bad Sandy in me is a bad influence. I can't get him in trouble again.

As Maia and Blake hang the curtains to create our fake basement stage, Jonah leans in to me and asks, "Think you can help me practice again this week?" He extends his arms and sways from side to side.

I quickly shake my head. "Sorry, I've got to help Maia with her singing. The audition's next week."

He nods, but I can tell he's disappointed.

"But I'll see you at community service tomorrow," I promise, glad that Charles and Amos spend so much time talking that Jonah and I barely get a chance.

"Sure. See you then."

A few minutes later, the scene is set and costumes are on. Maia wears a cute purple dress that her mom gave her for special occasions, and her hair is pulled back in a bun. I'm wearing my best suit with a white button-down. A crumpled white dishrag dangles from my collar, the closest to princely ruffles we can accomplish on our zero-dollar budget. Michal wears one of Jonah's suits from a few years ago with a matching dishrag.

Our star inhales deeply and releases a "Hee hee ha ha hi ho hum" on the exhale, just like Miss H. taught us. With a hand on her stomach, her back straight, she recites, "Red leather, purple pleather, hen feather, sweater weather." Her tongue flaps dramatically with each word.

Jonah and Blake get ready to film as Maia continues her rhyming warm-ups. "Help me out here, Calvin," she says. "Red leather, yellow leather, wonder whether good together?"

I smile. She's really good at this. "Maroon baboons can croon cartoon show tunes."

Maia leans forward and whispers, "You know I know rainbow heart glow?"

My face flushes. Why would she say that to me? "Uh . . . wrong song, ding dong."

"Knock knock, bawk-bagawk, you and me, let's talk."

"No go, cookie dough."

"All right," Jonah says, thankfully oblivious to my side chat with Maia. "Shall we shoot this thing?"

We take our places: Michal sprawled face-first on the floor, Maia and me side by side on the "stage." Blake starts rolling, and Jonah calls "Action!"

Maia's grin is so wide I can feel her cheeks pushing against mine as she holds out her phone to snap a selfie.

"You were ah-mazing, Melody," I rave as Johnny.

"You're sweet," she replies, reading the script from her phone screen since I didn't have time to print it out earlier. She covers by distractedly pretending to type a message to share along with the photo.

"Literal perfection. Kelvin really forked it up, but that just made you shine even brighter." We are both supposed to laugh at this, but I only hear myself.

"Forksooth," Michal says from the ground.

"I did what I could, given the circumstances." Maia should be saying this with contempt, but she brings almost no emotion to the scene. It's almost as if she doesn't want to do it.

"I wouldn't even be surprised if you felt like you had to take that agent's offer now, after Kelvin . . ." I wobble around to mimic falling off the stage. Somehow, I can't even say it out loud when I'm talking about a fictional someone else.

"I hope he's okay," Maia says, off script.

"What'd you write on your post?" I have Johnny say.

Maia checks out the words on her phone and shakes her head. "Calvin."

"Johnny," I correct.

"Calvin," she repeats more firmly. "I am not reading this."

"Let me see." I yank the phone from her hands and pretend to read the message Kennedy posted all those months ago on the night of the school show, as if I haven't memorized it by now. *"Despite everything, a true star always sparkles. Cheers to my new fall-owers."* My throat catches, and my eyes water as I read the final word of her post. *"Forsooth."*

"She didn't actually post that, did she?" Blake asks. His voice and posture are ready to fight. I notice the camera down by his side. We're going to have to reshoot the whole scene.

I wait for Jonah to call out "Action" so we can start again, but instead he says, "I think we're done here, Cal. For good."

Is he serious? Only one scene left to go, and suddenly our film's production is suspended.

CHAPTER 25

That night, there's a tap on my bedroom window. I promised Blake's dad I wouldn't get him in trouble again, plus I'm still devastated that Blake and Maia let Jonah give up on the film so easily. It's almost like they agreed with him. I text Blake from behind the closed blinds that I'm truly exhausted. I look at the clock on my phone that says 7:30 and wonder if he's buying it.

He taps again.

I close my eyes, lean back, and smush my head into my pillow. He'll go away in a minute.

The tapping continues.

"You gonna get that?" Sarah finally whines through the wall, and my face flushes.

I hop to the window and raise the blinds, fully prepared to tell my friend to go home, but when I notice the patches of pink circling his eyes, I can see that something's wrong. "Have you been crying?" I blurt out.

"Can I come in?"

I open the window and the screen. He places his hands on the windowsill and pulls himself up.

"Are you all right? What's going on?"

"My dad's having a panic attack," he says.

"Oh my God! Is he okay?"

"My mom's handling it. I had to get out of there."

"Are you going to get in trouble again?" I ask.

He shrugs. "If they find out." It's clear he doesn't care, so maybe I shouldn't either.

"Don't you want to be there for him too?"

"I am so tired of being there for people. For once, can't someone be there for me?"

I feel a twinge of guilt. It seems like I'm the someone—or at least, *a* someone—who should be there for him right now. "I'm sorry," I say. We stand in silence for a moment, me wearing a vivid coat of guilt. His stormy eyes search for my soul as he takes a seat on my bed.

After a while, Blake continues, "I really do like hanging out with you, Calvin, but I've got stuff too, and sometimes I'm not sure you care. You know you've never even come over to my house before."

"Actually, I did," I correct. "Your dad wouldn't let me inside."

I don't know what else to say since he's usually the one who comforts me. How can I say how much I care without saying how much I'm *afraid* I might care, especially with my parents literally down the hall? I sit beside him and consider stroking the screeching cat scrawled across his knuckles in black ink, but that doesn't feel right at all.

Finally, I find the courage to admit, "I care—"

KNOCK, KNOCK. "Calvin?" my mom says from the other side of my bedroom door.

"Just a second!" I call, hoping my panic is not audibly detectable. I turn to Blake and whisper, "Hide."

His expression says *Seriously?* but he burrows into a stack of laundry on the floor beside my bed. I throw a few more shirts and a blanket on top of him. This is a horrible disguise, but it's all we've got.

I open the door to find Mom and the General in the hallway, my mother clutching my yearbook to her chest. "Can we talk for a second?"

I nod, unable to even articulate words as the memory of the last day of school comes flooding back.

"Let's have a seat," my dad suggests, striding to my

bed and sitting in the spot Blake occupied moments ago. I wonder if he can feel Blake's warmth.

"What's up?" I ask, sitting next to my dad. My mom settles in on my other side.

"I was looking at your yearbook," she begins. I haven't looked at that thing since Blake passed it to my mom through the window at the beginning of summer. I wonder what's wrong with my picture, but when she flips it open, it's not to the black-and-white photographs. It's the autograph page. There, in smudged blue ink, is a single signature.

"*Remember to breathe. XO Blake,*" I read aloud. "That's great advice," I tell my parents.

"And it's the only piece of advice anyone left at all," Mom says.

"My other friends signed . . ." I trail off before I accidentally reveal the second, shredded yearbook. "Something else."

"We didn't even know you were friends with Blake at that point."

I try not to look at Blake disguised as a pile of laundry, instead focusing on the scratchy handwriting. We had barely spoken before then and he helped me. He didn't have to. He wanted to. Now he has stuff too, and I didn't even notice.

"What is your problem with him?" I ask Mom. "What piece of gossip could you and your friends have possibly uncovered that has you clutching your rosaries every time I mention the one person who has made me feel like I might not be a total disaster?" I hope Blake is hearing this and understanding how much I appreciate him.

Dad grimaces. "Calvin, you're not a—"

"It's his father," Mom interrupts. "You should've heard how rude he was to our Welcome Committee."

"Your problem with Blake is his dad? The man who's too afraid to open his door for a kid didn't want the Bible Study's homemade lasagna? Real *Love thy neighbor* energy, Mom." I picture Blake's dad at home now, caught in the middle of a panic attack. "He's struggling worse than I am. We should be helping him, not judging him."

"You spoke to him?" Mom says, horror creeping into her voice.

"And you haven't." It's not a question. "Can't you please fuh-reaking trust me for once?"

"We want to," Dad says.

"Then do it," I beg, rising to my feet. A hundred ants parade down my spine as the guilt of that movie outing returns. I don't deserve his trust, but

Blake doesn't deserve his *dis*trust. "Can't you be glad I have a friend who's helping me? Who wants me to breathe? Like, is that the worst thing in the world? No. Because you know what would be worse? If somebody moved in next door and needed a friend because he had stuff going on, really intense stuff, but nobody in town stepped up because they were too caught up in their own little worlds to even notice."

I gasp for air, shocked that I was brave enough to say what I said, and bracing myself for the fallout.

Mom is stunned silent. Dad opens his mouth to respond, and I see him glance toward the pile of clothes on the floor. I need to shut this down.

"Can we talk more later?" I ask, forcing out a breathy yawn. "I'm tired."

"Okay," Dad agrees. I'm surprised he doesn't put up more of a fight, but maybe he's too overwhelmed with fresh disappointment in me. He and Mom rise to their feet.

Before Dad exits, though, he grips my shoulder. He's staring at my pile of living laundry when he warns, "Cal, we're not angry at you, but it's hard to trust someone who hides so much from their parents. You need to trust us too. Understood?" It feels like he knows exactly what's lying underneath those clothes, but if he does, why is he ignoring it?

"Yes, sir," I reply.

"And you're helping with the wash tomorrow. It's a mess in here."

"Oh, I can grab that now," Mom says.

"No!" Dad and I both exclaim at the same time. His eyes lock with mine for a moment before darting back to the mound of dirty clothes. "He can do his own laundry for that little outburst."

"Okay," I promise as he releases me. "Night, Dad. Night, Mom."

"Good night," they say in unison, closing the door behind them.

Within seconds, Blake resurfaces, gasping for air. "Dang, that blanket really smells like you," he says with a laugh. I can't tell if he thinks that's a good thing or a bad thing. I shuffle over to lock the door in case my parents decide they haven't tormented me enough this evening.

"I'm sorry—" I begin to say, but before I can finish, he pulls me into a hug.

When he steps back, I add, "It's really unfair of my parents to think badly of you."

He shrugs. "Honestly, it's kind of nice they care

so much." I realize what that implies about his parents, and I wonder what's going on at his house right now. "I'm ready to listen," I promise.

Blake and I talk for hours. About his stuff. About mine.

The panic attacks were less frequent for a while after they moved, but his dad has been struggling for a couple months now. Blake started seeing a new therapist once they left the city, and they haven't connected in the same way he did with his previous one. Soon, he hopes. The only thing that's given him some comfort lately is our film. He's always wanted to make a movie with Real Actors.

"She really is kind of awful, though," Blake says, kicking off his flip-flops and repositioning on my bed so he's stretched out, leaning against my pillows. "If she's anything like Melody Monarchy."

Friendships aren't supposed to be this hard, Sarah's voice echoes in my mind. I frown. "Kennedy can be . . . a lot to handle, but nobody even looked at me before she did. And even though I'll never be as good as her, she pretended I was, and she's a really good actress, so sometimes, I even believed it."

"I believe it too," Blake says.

My cheeks prickle.

He continues, "We should give Kelvin a satisfying ending in the movie. Make him into a star. He deserves it."

I want to hug Blake right there because that is the nicest thing he could possibly say, and because suddenly, our movie is back on.

After a while, the talking gives way to a tired quiet. I don't know the correct way to ask a guest if he is going to leave, so we lie in silence, until that silence is replaced by Blake's gentle snoring, and I realize this is my very first home sleepover. Mom never allowed them with Jonah, mainly because she certainly couldn't allow them with Kennedy, and what's two-thirds of a best friend trio besides incomplete?

I throw a blanket over both of us, click off the light beside my bed, and listen to Blake's heavy breathing in the darkness. I wonder if I should wake him and tell him his parents might be worried, but it feels like that's not what he needs right now, so I let him sleep.

I scooch down farther into the bed and pull the covers up to my chin even though it's a million degrees in here. It feels like I'm sweating in the spotlight, and I'm afraid that oh-so-pleasant smell that sometimes follows may wake up my friend and scare him away. *Get it together, Calvin*, I scold myself. My body trembles at how absolutely uncool I am, and in the involuntary cringe, my foot taps the top of Blake's. It's colder than I expect, and it makes me shiver again.

I should pull my foot away from his, but I leave it there, occasionally wiggling my toes across the top to remind myself he's still here. I put all my attention on that single point of contact between us, because if I focus on my stomach, jittering in fear of being caught on an unapproved sleepover, I might scream.

Gradually, his foot doesn't feel so cold, and as I finally drift to sleep, the room doesn't feel so hot.

CHAPTER 26

I wake up to a persistent *tap-tap-tap* on my bedroom door. We are busted.

"Wake up," I whisper to Blake, but when I roll over—after wiping an unflattering string of drool from the corner of my lips—I realize he's already gone. The window and screen are wide open, and Blake is nowhere to be seen.

"Gimme a sec," I call toward the door as I fluff up his pillow to make it look unused. When I'm sure the coast is clear, I push off the covers and lumber to the door. Prepared to fend off Mom, I'm surprised to find—"Jonah?"

He seems equally flustered to see me, and I become very aware of my bedhead and rumpled clothes. I shoot my hand up and do my best to flatten the mane. Compared to him, in some freshly ironed khakis and a partly tucked-in button-down that looks a little warm for late July, I'm a real slob.

"What are you doing here?" I ask.

Sarah jangles down the hallway, car keys in hand, also looking very School Picture Day. "Brush your teeth and put on some slacks," she instructs as she passes by. "We're leaving in five."

"Community service," he says, staring past me at my open window. "Did you forget?"

"Oh right, right, right, right, right," I say. "Hold on." I grab a pair of pants and dash to the bathroom, stopping for a moment to slam my window screen shut.

Jonah says nothing the whole ride. At the community center, instead of spending time with Amos and Charles, he holes up in the kitchen washing dishes alone. It reminds me of when I first fell off the stage and he couldn't get far enough away from me. I thought we were past that now.

"Where's our boy?" Amos asks after they've beaten me at checkers three times. "He knows how to play."

I pretend not to be insulted, even though it hurts a little. "I think he's mad at me."

"Well, that's no good," says Amos. "You gonna patch things up with him?" I've heard that wisdom comes with age, so it's no surprise that these guys immediately know that it is all my fault.

"I want to," I say. "Hypothetically, if somebody was in love with one of you but she thinks the two of you are in love with each other because you accidentally said something that made her think so and she explodes, what would you do?"

Charles and Amos exchange a glance.

"Is it true?" Charles asks.

"It's hypothetical."

"Well, hypothetically," Amos replies, "I'd talk to Jonah."

I know Jonah comes here a little more often than I do for his mitzvah project, but I didn't realize he'd become a confidant to Charles and Amos. At least he's talking to someone.

"Why don't you go get him?" Amos suggests.

"Okay," I say, rising to my feet.

I push into the kitchen and find Jonah with his back to me, a stack of sudsy pots in front of him. His hands, buried inside adult-sized, yellow rubber gloves, frantically scrubbing.

"Jonah?" I place my hand on his shoulder.

He shudders and doesn't even turn to face me. "Sup?"

"The guys want you to join us. They're killing me."

He swipes his nose with a yellow-gloved hand that I can only imagine smells like soggy leftovers. "You are pretty bad," he admits, which, rude.

When he turns to face me, I see a strain of tears stretching down each of his brown cheeks.

"What's wrong?" I ask, extending my hand to take his because friends hold friends' hands all the time. I only pause when I remember those rubber gloves he's still wearing and the message I accidentally sent to Kennedy.

"Wrong?" he says. "Why would anything be wrong?"

I sigh with relief. Maybe I've been imagining things, projecting things onto him . . .

"It was so great seeing Blake escape from your window when I pulled up this morning. Love that excluded feeling."

My heart plummets down my body and through the red-orange tile floor. "Let me explain . . ."

"Save it, Calvin. Let me guess. You're surprising me with a film, so you've decided to shut me out too?" He throws off his gloves and tosses them onto the counter beside the sink. They make a *thwack* sound that slaps like Jonah's words. "You know, it's one thing when friends grow apart. My mom says that can happen and it's not necessarily anyone's fault. But it's another thing to be flat-out rejected. Now Kennedy's blocked me, and—"

"She blocked you too?" My eyes widen. She actually thinks that things are *things* with Jonah and me, which is ridiculous because he can barely even look at me right now. I have to convince her that Jonah and I are two-thirds of a broken friend group, nothing more. "I messed up," I admit.

Jonah doesn't tell me I'm perfect. Instead he stares at me hard. "What'd you do?"

"I told her about the dancing."

"You what?"

"She got the wrong idea, and she blocked us. But if we can explain to her that it was all a mistake, a misunderstanding . . ."

"Great. Sure. A mistake." His voice sounds hollow. "And now we're gonna lose her completely."

"The film will redeem us!" I say. "We just need to finish it. One more scene and she'll know exactly how we feel about her. It'll be the most moving piece of cinema—"

"Fine. Whatever." He wipes the tears from beneath each eye. "But if this doesn't work, it's on you."

He pushes past me, on his way to play a game of checkers with our elderly friends.

I don't think he wants me to follow him, so I turn to the disgusting stack of dishes. I feel awful, but I also cling to a glimmer of hope.

Jonah wants to win Kennedy back. He's rejoining the film too.

CHAPTER 27

The day of the church solo auditions has arrived.

"Good luck, hon," Mom says in a singsong voice when we roll to a stop in front of the church.

"Thanks," I manage, though I'm not nervous for the reason she thinks. Now that I've got our director and cinematographer on board with finishing the film, I just need to get my lead back. I need to get Maia this solo.

Inside, Father Paul is standing with a notebook and pen in hand. "You ready, Calvin?" he asks with an obvious wink.

"Maia's been working really hard," I reply, doing my best to fulfill my end of a pointless promise.

"And you?" His head tips down and his glasses scoot down his nose a little, zooming in on me. "I thought *you* wanted to be a star."

My heart jumps, because I do, but I know this is a trick. I recite what Father Paul himself said to me earlier this summer: "We're not here to be stars, sir. We're here for Him." I nod toward the outstretched arms of Jesus.

"Touché," he says with a chuckle.

It's easier to laugh along than to tell him that I don't speak French, so I fake a laugh that booms throughout the church. All eyes turn to me, and I realize I might have overdone it. Father Paul suppresses a sigh before rushing over to Ms. Clarkson at her piano. I can almost hear my acting mentor Kennedy scold, *Take it down three notches, Cal.*

Maia strides over and links her arm through mine, squeezing a little too tight. "What was that about?"

"I was putting in a good word for you," I tell her.

She immediately loosens her grip and tilts her head sideways to lean on my shoulder.

"All right, kids," Father Paul says from the piano. He claps his hands to get everyone's attention. "Here we are. The moment we've all been waiting for. The summer solo!"

Maia squeezes my arm again. I wriggle free.

"Now, each of you has one minute to wow us. When I call your name, head to the front, tell us your song, and begin." Father Paul pulls out an iPhone, which I never even thought a priest would have. "I'll be timing you." His eyes turn to the choir as he says, "Adriana?"

One of the high schoolers rises to her feet. "I will be singing 'Ave Maria.'" She sounds fine, but even if this thing wasn't rigged for me, she honestly would have no chance compared to Maia. Plus, talk about cliché. Why would anyone pick "Ave Maria" when you could choose something from the musical theater songbook?

I lean into Maia. "You've got this," I lie.

"Stop," Father Paul calls out. I almost think he's yelling at me, but then he waves his phone in the air. "Thank you, Adriana," he says. "Jonathan?" Some sophomore rises to his feet. When he starts to sing about the city of God, I realize that Father Paul will be calling *everyone*. Even the people who don't want the solo. Even the one who has already been promised the song. I've been so worried about pretending that Maia has a chance and helping her practice that I haven't thought about what *I'll* sing.

Jonathan sings for his allotted minute, followed by Aimee, Mary Something (Grace maybe?), Rebecca, and Maia. As expected, Maia is the true standout.

"I will be singing 'Climb Ev'ry Mountain' from *The Sound of Music*," she announces to the group. I was so excited when I remembered this song that could perfectly represent Kennedy/Melody reaching for her dreams, while still sounding pretty darn Godly.

She begins to sing, and it is even more glorious than she sounded during our rehearsals. Her voice does things I didn't know were possible.

I've got chills, and only about 50 percent of those chills are because I have no idea what I'm supposed to do when it's my turn to sing or how I'm going to save our film if Father Paul still gives me the solo after this.

The priest shows almost no emotion as he interrupts the angel at her finest moment with a rude "Stop." Maia scoots back to my side and I realize there's only one singer left.

Wait a second. Father Paul can't give the solo to someone who doesn't try out.

"I've got to go," I whisper to Maia, rising to my feet to hide in the bathroom. I creep away with my back hunched over, making myself as invisible as possible.

"Calvin," Father Paul says.

I freeze.

My back straightens. All eyes turn to me.

I turn to face the priest and gulp before confidently stating, "Pass." I scramble back to my seat beside Maia.

Some of the high schoolers chuckle. Father Paul is staring at me, but I refuse to lock eyes with him. Maia deserves this solo, and now I've handed it to her.

"You're welcome," I whisper to Maia, hoping this scheme works.

"As if I wouldn't have crushed you anyway." She shoves my shoulder playfully.

Father Paul walks over to Ms. Clarkson. They whisper for a few minutes. When his back straightens and he turns to face the choir, Maia grabs my hand and squeezes.

"Thank you, everyone, for your auditions today. They gave us a lot to think about and after some discussion, we've decided the solo will go to . . ." Father Paul's eyes scan the crowd until he finds me. I realize my plan did not work an agonizing second before he announces, "Calvin."

Maia's grip tightens as she exclaims what everyone else is thinking: "What?!"

"I swear to God, Calvin!" Maia screams at me on the front lawn of the church.

"And maybe that's why Father Paul didn't give you the part," I say, lifting my arms to my head protectively. "Swearing to God is—"

"No," she barks back. "I didn't get the part because you chose a garbage song, tricked me into singing it, and meanwhile got all buddy-buddy with the priest."

"I thought you liked the song!"

"That's not the point!"

"I tried to convince Father Paul to give you the solo. I begged him not to pick me for it. You have to believe me!"

Maia lets out a drawn-out groan. "I'm sorry, but you have to understand how this feels."

I nod, because I've never been a lead either, and can't we celebrate that for like one second?

"It's like . . ." She inhales through her nose. "It's like, another undeserving white kid taking a role that I worked so hard for, that should belong to me. First Kennedy. Now you."

My heart plummets. "But I didn't do anything."

"Exactly," she groans. "You didn't do anything and you still got the part. And here I am, humiliating myself in this ridiculous film of yours to prove to

236

you all that I'm good enough." She's nearly crying. "But you know what? I'm not just good enough. I'm better. And even though this whole stinkin' town doesn't get it, that doesn't mean it's not true."

"You're right," I admit. "You're so good, and you deserve so much better. When Father Paul told me he was giving the solo to me after I set the church on fire, I thought we could change his mind—"

"Wait," she says, holding up a finger. "He gave you the solo after you set the church on fire? Like *right* after?"

All I can get out is an "Uhhhh" that tells Maia everything.

"You lied to me all summer? Why? To keep me in your little film? To save your *real* friendship?"

"I'm sorry! I didn't know what else to do!"

"You are unbe-freaking-lievable, Calvin." She swipes at her cheek. "I quit."

"Quit? But—hang on—"

"Let me say it a little slower. Your. Film. Is. Finished. I. Quit."

As she marches across the parking lot and slips into her grandmother's car, the curtain falls on my newest friendship, and the lights go out on the one I'd hoped she could help save.

KENNEDY

It probably doesn't help, but you're
not the only one who hates me now

I messed up again

I ruined everything

Why do I keep doing this?

How am I supposed to fix it?

It's me, Calvin, by the way,
in case you deleted my number

Kennedy, I need you

Sent.

CHAPTER 28

Sarah is supposed to pick me up after practice, but she's late. Probably off canoodling with Anthony, leaving me with plenty of time to fix this for Maia. The rest of the choir exited the building stage left during Maia's and my big blowup, their scowls at me and nods at Maia confirming that they all hate me too. Even Ms. Clarkson scooted off in her boxy blue car, which means Father Paul is alone inside. Perfect.

I swing the wooden door open and march straight to the priest's office. It's a little creepy being in here all by myself. I know the Holy Spirit isn't the haunting sort of ghost, but if it were, I'll be very easy to find with my heart thumping so loudly.

When I get to the office doorway, I encounter something even more frightening. "Ahhhhh!"

I scream at the sight of Father Paul in jeans and a T-shirt. Is this what happens when a priest loses one of his usual uniforms to an accidental inferno? Am I to blame for this abomination?

He covers his ears. "Sheesh, Calvin, what is going on? I thought everyone had left."

Taking a deep breath, I say, "Maia deserves that solo."

"Deserves? That song was not from any hymn-book I've ever seen."

"She has the voice of an angel," I argue, ignoring the disrespect for Rogers and Hammerstein. "And I didn't . . ."

"You didn't even try." He crosses his arms. "Why not?"

"I didn't want it."

"I don't believe that."

There's a pause as he studies me, and I wonder if he actually went to the University of Alaska as his T-shirt implies, or if he's a big fan of their sports teams. Or maybe priests get their casual clothes from charities. Before I can ask, he says, "I think you're afraid."

I feel light-headed. I want to snap back, but I know Mom would kill me if I lost my manners with a priest. "Afraid of what?" I ask, trying to be as polite-ish as possible.

"I have something for you," he says as he rummages through a drawer in his desk. "I was going to give you this at the next rehearsal, but since you're here now . . ." He pulls out a loose sheet of paper and hands it to me.

"What's this?" I ask, not even bothering to read it.

"The summer solo," he replies.

"Great. I'll pass it on to Maia."

"I'm sorry, Calvin. My decision was final when we spoke in June. It's what we agreed on. You weren't lying to a priest back then, were you?"

I cannot answer that question honestly without making God a little mad, so I say nothing.

"I chose this song specifically for you," Father Paul continues. I can't help but wonder how he knows my key when I didn't even try out. "In a few weeks, the stage will be yours. And not only are you going to wow us all, but this song is going to help you too."

I swear this man should be a salesman, because all I can say is "Thank you, sir." Clutching the sheet to my chest, I quickly retreat from the church. When I'm outside, I finally glance down at the sheet and read the song's title: "Be Not Afraid."

I rescan the parking lot. Sarah is still nowhere to be found, so I decide to walk home.

I'm fine. I'm fine. I'm fine, I repeat to myself with each step, trying so hard to believe it.

When I'm almost home, Blake pops out of the front door of his house, stopping me in my tracks. "Calvin?" he asks, and something about the concern in his voice makes me realize I may look much less fine than I'm pretending to be. "What's wrong?"

"I got the church solo," I reply. "So Maia quit our movie. And she thinks I'm racist."

His eyes bug out a little. "She said that?"

I try to remember what she actually said. "Well, more like she called the whole town racist. She called *me* undeserving. And I don't know if she's wrong." Blake said it himself. Other people have stuff, and I'm too selfish to notice. "She really *should* have gotten the solo, but Father Paul says it has to be me."

The sheet music crinkles in my pocket with each step, reminding me that I kind of almost want it now. The song is called "Be Not Afraid." It sounds like exactly what I need because I'm afraid all the time. I inhale through my nose, quick sniffly breaths that become increasingly frantic.

It's fine. It's fine. It's fine. This church song is going to make everything better, except for the rift it caused with Maia that left a huge gap in the film that Jonah is counting on to repair his relationship with Kennedy that he desperately needs since he thinks I'm replacing him with Blake even though I ruined our friendship long before we knew Blake by falling off the stage, which is of course why Kennedy left town, and if Blake sees me cry again here, he's going to think I'm a selfish loser who leans on him too much even though he has stuff too, and I can't tell him how he makes me feel like a rainbow parade because if Mom and Dad knew they'd think Blake was an even worse influence than they already do, but if Blake is such a bad influence why is he the only one who knows how to calm me down or who cares enough to try?

Without warning, my knees buckle, and I collapse face first onto Blake's front lawn.

"Calvin!" I can hear the thud of his bare feet on the dirt as Blake races up to me.

I start sobbing. I close my eyes, sucking in the scent of grass. A blade tickles my nostril with each snotty sniff.

Those familiar hands find my shoulders, their

warmth burning through my back and burrowing into my heart. "It's okay, Calvin. Breathe."

I try to suck in some air and inhale some dirt, which makes me cough.

Blake grips my shoulder and rolls me over. I lie on my back while he pulls his phone out of his pocket. "I'm calling your mom."

My spine tightens. "Please don't," I manage to get out, even though I don't think he has her number. She could probably see us if she happened to look out a window, though. What would her friends say if they could see me now?

I open my mouth and take a bite of the air, as if it's possible to eat oxygen. It seems to help, and soon I'm down to a steady pant. I'm suddenly aware that Blake's hand is now on my chest, and the warmth instantly spreads up to my cheeks and down toward my knees. I prop myself up onto my elbows. "I just need a second."

"A second to bury your face in the ground like an ostrich?" He stuffs his phone into his pocket and raises his hand up to brush some grass off my cheek. His fingers glide through my hair, fluffing it up and flicking away the dead grass.

Before I can think better of it, my hand shoots up and finds his. Our fingers touch.

He studies me with that crooked grin that usually brings out a smirk in me too, but all I can think about is how I've ruined everything. "I can't lose another friend," I whisper.

He guides our intertwined hands down so they hover between us. "You haven't lost any."

I wish I could agree. "No movie means Kennedy will never know how we feel, which means she'll never forgive Jonah, which means Jonah will never forgive *me*, and I literally lied to Maia all summer for nothing."

"We'll fix this," he promises. We both stare at our tangled fingers. "Together." The gentle squeeze convinces me that maybe he's right.

A car rolls to a stop behind Blake. It beeps twice. Sarah leans out the window and says, "What the heck, Calvin?"

My hand thrusts forward to push Blake's away as I wonder what exactly Sarah saw.

"Sorry." Blake shrugs. "I had to text someone."

I rise shakily to my feet and somehow manage to wobble to my sister's car so she can drive us one house down. As I swing open the car door, Blake calls out behind me, "*I'll* do it."

I whip around to face him, and he seems almost

nervous. Like he regrets whatever decision he's made. "Do what?"

"I'll play Melody."

I ask, "What?" as Sarah laughs out loud.

I think he's serious. My eyes scrunch as I scan Blake, trying to picture him looking anything like Maia as Melody Monarchy.

"Listen," he says. "We have just one scene left. We'll shoot from far away, and I can do some fancy editing stuff. Maia herself will never know the difference."

My mind races, making a hundred excuses for why this isn't a good idea, but Blake really thinks it'll be okay, and he hasn't let me down all summer.

"You're on," I tell him, climbing into Sarah's car and wishing I was still holding his hand.

CHAPTER 29

"Where's Maia?" Jonah asks as Blake and I arrive at the location for our final scene: the train station. I pull a couple of suitcases out of Sarah's trunk and slam it closed. Anthony and Sarah pull away, leaving us alone with Jonah and Michal. It's almost eerie here with no passengers around. We must be way before the next train.

"Maia's not coming," I explain. My eyes dart toward the duffel bag draped over Blake's shoulder.

Jonah's gaze follows. "What, does he have like a ventriloquist dummy in there?"

"Stuffed chicken?" Michal guesses.

I laugh, because that would be hilarious. Blake smirks too. "Nah," I say, "but we've got a plan."

Blake reaches out to hand Jonah his camera. His arms have been scrubbed clean. I can barely see the smudged black ink. "You're on filming duty today," he says. With both hands now free, he unzips the duffel bag and pulls out a grass-green sweatshirt and a ratty, lime-green witch wig. He pulls on the sweatshirt and throws the wig on top of his head. It all clashes with the army-green gym shorts he's already wearing. It's such a strange contrast to his usual black wardrobe. To top it off, he puts on a pair of sunglasses and a wide-brimmed, floppy hat that he must have stolen from his mom. Melody's travel attire is as oversized as Kennedy's spirit.

"Little green-screen computer magic, and *BAM!* Melody," I explain to Jonah and Michal.

"No," Jonah says immediately, turning his back on the whole scene and walking away. "Absolutely not."

"Hey, wait!" I chase after Jonah, throwing my arms around his chest from behind. He tries to wiggle free, but he can't escape my grasp. It's like the yearbook battle all over again, which is perfect to set the mood for this final scene.

"We have to do this," I insist.

"Why, Calvin? Why is Blake our one option to replace Maia?"

"You know I don't have any other friends."

"I could do it," Michal pipes up from behind.

"We need you for Kelvin's big finale," Blake says. My heart doesn't miss the fact that he actually followed through and insisted I write Calvin—I mean, Kelvin—a happy ending.

My chin is practically resting on Jonah's shoulder as I say into his ear, "Don't you want Kennedy to forgive us?"

"You really think this is the most flattering way to honor her?" He points toward Blake, who's pacing along the platform, flipping his green hair from side to side as he channels his inner diva.

"Hee hee ho ho hey hi hum," Blake mutters to himself as he releases a deep, nervous breath. And he said he wasn't an actor.

Jonah is not so easily charmed. "Why don't you call Mai—"

"She quit, Jonah. I got the church solo and she quit."

He almost sounds proud when he asks, "You got the solo?"

"I messed up another friendship. I need this." I whisper into his ear, "I need you." I catch a whiff of his scent and am brought back to his basement, dancing. I quickly release him.

Jonah groans, but his "Fine" sounds more pleased

than I think he intends. It seems he finally understands the genius behind this plan as he calls out, "Places."

Blake scoops up the suitcases and heads up the platform. I reach into the duffel bag to pull out both halves of the torn yearbook that Jonah and I destroyed on the last day of school. I've taped a fake Playbill cover onto the front. I hand both parts to Michal as Jonah raises the camera. When the red light clicks on, he goes, "Action!"

"Melody, wait!" Michal calls out as Kelvin. We both race up to our star. "What's this about a secret message in your Playbill autograph?"

Blake looks down at us from above his sunglasses. "Please don't read it here," he whimpers. His fake high-pitched voice really sounds nothing like Maia, so I hope his audio editing skills are as good as his green screening.

"Let me see that," I say as Johnny.

"No! It's mine!" Michal keeps her grip on the fake Playbill, and we pantomime a tug-of-war until finally it rips apart.

I look at the half in my hand and flip it open. I pretend to read the line that Blake insisted I add to the script: *"My dearest Kelvin, I cannot believe you won a local Tony. The Rising Star Award. What did I tell you? The curtain cannot rise if it's never fallen down. I was right about you all along. I know this is just the beginning for you.*"

"I won?" Michal looks a mix of honored and moved. "Why was this a secret?"

"Keep reading," our new Melody says.

I do: "*I'm only sorry I won't be there to share the stage with you next time.*"

"You're still leaving?" I ask.

Michal pretends to faint.

Blake-as-Melody looks me directly in the eyes and asks, "Is there a reason to stay?"

I look at Blake, thinking of Kennedy and the one thing that could possibly convince her to stay here. "What about me? Can't I be your reason?"

Jonah gapes at us from behind the camera.

"Then you know how I feel?" Blake-as-Melody says.

I nod.

"And you?" he asks timidly. He has removed the fake voice, sounding exactly like regular Blake.

I nod again. A real tear escapes from my eye because this scene is killer. The drip of water runs down my cheek, thankfully on the camera's side.

I hope this taped-up little box we're calling a camera records in HD.

Blake-as-Melody cups his palm on my cheek and pushes the tear away with his thumb. He keeps his hand there, staring at me through his large sunglasses. His grayish-blue eyes beneath are also watering. There is so much fear in them. Fear of losing Johnny. Fear of giving up her big chance. Now this is Acting!

That's when Blake, completely caught up in the scene, leans in and kisses me. I'm surprised because I assumed this part was going to be added with green screen special effects, but I'm also an actor, so I kiss him back. Blake-as-Melody's hands wrap around my back and pull me closer. I know this is the best scene I've ever acted in my entire life because my whole body is tingling. I mean literally, my *whole* body.

Jonah calls out "Cut!" but we don't cut. This is the ending we need. I have no idea what I'm doing as I bring my hand to Blake-as-Melody's cheek, tucking it between his ear and the green wig. My fingers curl around the back of his head, wrapping around his short spiky hair tucked beneath.

"I SAID CUT!" Jonah screams. I know I should for so many reasons, I really know it, but I don't until

I somehow manage to push Blake's wig off of his head. It flops onto the platform along with his hat.

I step back, still shaking. Blake seems just as breathless as I am.

Michal's mouth has dropped open. "Whoa," she says, which gives me Oscar hopes.

Jonah's eyes dart from Blake to me to Blake to me. "What was that? I . . . you . . ." He trails off.

Did Blake and I really do *that* in front of Jonah and Michal? "We can . . ." I take a breath, struggling to speak. "We can edit before the wig falls off." I glance toward Blake, who's fiddling with the left cuff of his sweatshirt. "Right?"

He nods and gives me a thumbs up.

"Are you serious?" Jonah snaps. "I . . . I . . . I . . ." his voice is quivering. "I have to get out of here." He throws the camera to the ground. It lands on the pavement with a crack that snaps me out of my haze.

"Hey!" Blake snaps as he races over to check out the damage to his prized possession. Jonah doesn't hear or doesn't care. He's already halfway gone, tugging Michal along behind him.

CHAPTER 30

As Blake kneels and fumbles with the camera, I scoop our stuff into the duffel bag. "I'll be right back," I promise.

He gives me his crooked smile that I now know tastes like lip balm. I bite my own lips, which taste like his. What have I done?

I chase after Jonah, stopping for only a second to grab half a yearbook that Michal left behind.

One thing about Jonah: he's fast when he wants to be. It's those tap classes that Mom and Dad insisted weren't for me. He's already gone a block and a half before I'm able to catch up to him running my fastest.

"Jonah, wait!" I beg. He finally halts in his tracks. Michal nearly crashes into her brother. His voice is tough when he places his hand on her shoulder. I see that it's shaking. "Go on ahead," he tells her. "I'll be there in a second."

"Are you okay?" she asks

"I'm fine."

Michal reluctantly walks away.

Jonah doesn't say anything until he's sure his sister is out of earshot. The icy vibes his eyes shoot in my direction are like nothing I've seen before. I feel a literal chill.

He finally says, "You realize Maia talked about that solo all summer, right?"

"What does this have to do with Maia?"

"All you had to do was give it back to her, and this scene would have worked the way I wanted."

"With Kennedy moving away?"

"Exactly!" Jonah is beyond frustrated, but I know I've written the ending he needs.

"You're lying."

He snatches the yearbook from my hands. I flinch. It's like the last day of school all over again. He flips to the autograph section. I instantly catch Kennedy's flowery farewell, but he points instead to a smaller signature in the corner, in regular old blue pen.

Looks like just you and me next year. We're gonna

kill it. Love you, man. Jonah. I scan the message a few more times, because this doesn't make any sense. "You signed before Kennedy."

He nods.

"So you knew she was leaving?"

"She told me not to tell."

"And yet you pretended you didn't know what her note to me said, and you ended up destroying my yearbook over it."

Guilt creeps into his eyes. "I didn't mean to ruin your yearbook," he says quietly.

"Oh? So what—you just wanted to wrestle me or something?"

He pauses, clearly caught red-handed. "It's called acting," he finally says.

"Acting like my feelings don't matter?" I grab the yearbook back from him, scanning to see what scandals my other classmates revealed in their notes. There are like twenty *Have a nice summer*s, which approximately translate to *I don't really know you*. But then again, that's exactly how I feel about Jonah right now. "How long did you know?"

"That's not the point right now, Calvin."

"Oh, right!" I'm shouting now. "The point is that you were too busy avoiding me after I fell off the stage to be bothered to tell me that our best friend was leaving—"

"THE POINT IS"—Jonah stands on his tiptoes so that we're exactly the same height—"this is the Idolization of Kennedy all over again."

"What does that even mean?"

"Kennedy made you feel talentless so you would worship her. Now Blake tells you you're broken so he can 'fix' you. But you're not broken. You never were. I am so sick of seeing people manipulate you, trying to change you, trying make you believe you're someone you're not so they can swoop in and be your hero." His voice cracks as he adds, "So they can kiss you."

My back stiffens. "Excuse me," I bite back. "Kennedy kissed *you*. Not me."

"I'm not talking about Kennedy. I told you I'm not into her like that." The arch of his eyebrow disappears. He reaches out, and I shrink back. He places a hand on each of my shoulders. His grip is gentle but overwhelming. My heart thumps.

If we stuck out our tongues, I think they'd touch. Okay, why would I even think that? Especially after what just happened with Blake. My insides quake in the pre-roller-coaster kind of way. It's weird, but I find myself biting my tongue because a part of me *wants* to stick it out and see what happens. What is wrong with me? Roller-coasters make me sick. I feel the drips of sweat falling down my armpits.

"Who are you talking about then?" I manage to squeak out.

Jonah doesn't answer for the longest time. I remember what he said about not being able to speak his mind.

After a moment, Jonah says, "Let me put it this way. I don't like the new ending you wrote for the film." Great. Another critique of my writing. "You got it all wrong. Johnny is not in love with Melody. There was a crush, maybe, once, but he doesn't want to be with her now, or ever. She means a lot to him, he will never forget what she's done for him, he hopes they can still be friends one day, but he's . . . struggling to forgive her. He really, truly, wants her to go."

"And what do you want for Kelvin?" I can barely hear myself. If it weren't for my heart banging around inside of me, I would not be convinced that I was actually breathing right now.

"I want him to be honest with himself. I want him to see the truth." He shrugs and steps back. "And until he does, I need a moment."

A moment? For what?

"I gotta go," he says. He doesn't look at me again as he walks away.

My head starts to spin. I think Jonah just quit our friendship.

He's not in love with Kennedy. I don't think he ever will be. He got in my face to practically scream it at me. Right after Blake kissed me. My lips were still warm.

I glance toward the train station, too far to see from here. Is Blake still waiting for us to come back? Jonah's warnings rattle through my mind. Waiting to trick me. To change me. To kiss me. But if Blake is really using me, then why do I want to go back to the train station and practice the scene one more time to make sure we got it right? I bite the inside of my lip. The flavor of his lip balm is starting to fade.

It's called acting, it's called acting, it's called acting.

But Blake's not an actor, the tiny me in the red devil suit says.

And he looked so cute right before he kissed you, the little me in the angel robe and halo agrees.

Wait. You're supposed to be against this, I tell my imagined conscience.

He shrugs. *I'm just your thoughts.*

The world starts to spin. *Breathe, Calvin.* I know these are Blake's words, but he's not trying to change me. He's trying to help me. When nobody else would. *Breathe.*

My first kiss was with a boy. He maybe even did it on purpose, which means there might one day be a second or a third. My knees are about to buckle. I leap behind the nearest tree in case Blake heads this way looking for me, because I'm not sure I'm ready to face him. To face his face.

My fingers find their way to my mouth, rubbing off any remnants of Blake's.

I have to get out of here before he finds me. I pull my phone out of my pocket and text Sarah: Done early. Can you get me?

I wait, and I wait, and I wait.

Nothing.

"Cal?" Blake calls from down the street. I hear the wheels of the two suitcases rolling behind him. My back pushes tighter against the tree, the rough bark threatening to tear the fabric of my T-shirt. I hope I'm fully hidden from view on the sidewalk.

I wait a couple minutes after the sound of the wheels have passed before I peek again. He's gone past, maybe a block away. I can just make out the back of his head.

I pull out my phone: Nothing from Sarah, which means I'm walking the three miles home, one shaky step at a time.

CHAPTER 31

Blake's texted me like a hundred times:

Where are you?

Are you ok?

Did you go to Jonah's?

He's not texting me back either.

On my way there now.

I'm still not ready to talk to him, but I know one thing for sure: He absolutely cannot go to Jonah's right now.

I text back, Accidentally went home. Sorry.

The bouncing gray dots decide what he wants to say for a while before finally settling on Oh ok. I can read the sadness in those four little letters. If that kiss meant anything to him, well, I'm sure it doesn't now.

I begin to type something else, but I don't know what to say. Talking about what happened means it was something worth talking about. But it was only a movie, despite what Jonah and the little devil on my shoulder and my still-tingling lips have to say. I stuff my phone back into my pocket and remind myself to breathe and Be Not Afraid the whole walk home.

When I'm almost there, I realize I'm not ready to pass Blake's house in case he somehow got back before me, so I detour down a side street to approach my house from the other direction. It feels like a great idea until I nearly crash into Maia, riding a bike.

"Watch it, Calvin Conroy," she sneers as she slams on the brakes.

"Sorry," I manage to get out.

"Jeez," she says, "you look like you're a fugitive or something."

That's exactly what I am. A fugitive running from all my mistakes.

I fell off the stage.

I drove Kennedy away.

I lied to Maia all summer.

I hurt Jonah.

"I kissed Blake."

Maia's scowling mouth drops open. "No way."

Wait. Did I say that out loud?

She hops off her bike, and it clatters to the sidewalk. "What the heck did I miss?" she says, but with a different h-word that would make both of our mothers shudder.

Language, my mom's voice warns in my mind, which makes me think about what Mom and the General would have to say about everything. The guilt crawls over me like invisible spiders, pouring out of my chest and spreading in every direction. The ones in my brain tickle the back of my eyes, and my vision blurs. Breathe, Calvin, breathe, but I really can't. I can pretend I was Johnny and Blake was Melody, but I know whose lips they really were. I know how it made me feel. I know what my parents would say. I blubber as I imagine their broken hearts.

I brush away the tears and look at Maia. "I should go," I say before my recently kissed lips can spill any more. I spin in a dramatic circle and stride away.

"Calvin, hold up," Maia calls.

I can hear the footsteps slapping on the pavement behind me, but I can't let her comfort me. I lied to her all summer. She has stuff too, and I ignored it all until my latest crisis. I'm a horrible friend, and Maia doesn't deserve this mess.

I pick up the pace. Unfortunately, she does too.

"Can you stop for a second?" Maia begs. "Listen to me."

"I can hear you fine," I say with more quiver in my voice than I would like.

If I were looking at her, I imagine she'd be rolling her eyes and throwing her hands up in the air before giving up on me altogether, saying *You're not worth this, Calvin Conroy,* because we all know I'm not.

"My aunt is gay. My tía Julieta."

I stumble over my own feet. Like really, almost face-plant onto the sidewalk. I right myself and turn to face her. "That's great for her, Maia. Really, it is. You know how fine I am with it. But the kiss didn't mean—"

"She was sixteen when she told her parents," Maia continues. "And you know my family is religious like no other. She risked everything. And her dad—my abuelo—freaked out." Oh, great. Super helpful, Maia.

"That's exactly what my parents would do if, um, Sarah or someone told them she was gay. And that breaks my heart. For Sarah. Because I love my family. I mean, *she* does. And if my mom and dad weren't angry or disappointed enough before—"

"But here's the thing, Cal. My grandpa rejected her, but my grandma would have none of that. She knew God would want her to love her children, so she scooped up her two daughters and she left. She moved the family here because she believed in love. And ever since then, my aunt's been open about who she is, and the rest of our family is too. You can be who you are and still be loved."

My face is burning. I try to convince myself that it's only the sun.

"I know you've listened to all of *Kinky Boots* on low volume, Cal, but I want you to know it's okay to play it a little louder too." She leans in and hugs me. I hug back.

"Thank you," I whisper.

After a minute, she steps back. "I'm still mad about the solo," she adds sternly, "but I'm here for you. Okay?"

I nod. "Thanks."

We each wait a moment for the other to speak, but neither of us does. Finally, Maia scoops up her bike, and a moment later she's gone.

As I make my way home, there are a million scenes playing through my head, and try as I may, I cannot turn down the volume.

CHAPTER 32

I slam the front door behind me, hoping to trap all the noisy thoughts outside the house where they belong. I'm greeted by the pictures of Sarah and me, smiling down from an assortment of frames. Seeing them all, I can't help but picture Maia's aunt at sixteen, being kicked out by one parent while the other sacrificed everything for her.

Which would Mom be? What about Dad?

I'm halfway down the hall when Sarah's bedroom door bursts open. My sister storms out, followed closely by Mom. I press myself against the wall to avoid being trampled. I'm not even sure if they see me as they tear past.

"I am not done talking to you!" Mom shouts.

"Well, I'm done talking to you," Sarah says. "I have nothing else to say. He's a good guy. It's none of your business. You need to get over it."

It? What *it*? He me? Did they find out about the kiss? Could one of Mom's friends have been at the train station? I thought it was empty. Did Maia tell her mother?

Mom bellows, "We raised you kids to act a certain way."

I don't know how, but it's clear Mom found out what happened, and for some reason she is blaming my sister.

As much as I want to, I can't hide away in my room while my sister fights my battles for me, so I creep along behind them. Sarah retreats into the living room and turns on the TV as my mother hovers above her.

"Say something," Mom demands with such force that I almost shout *I'm sorry*.

My heart is throbbing in my chest, drowning in guilt for all the ways I've failed my parents. Rules, Responsibility, and Reputation all cast aside in one afternoon. I can't bring myself to check out the portrait of Jesus lurking behind me because I would not be surprised if He was sporting tiny painted tears today. Sarah does not deserve this. But am I ready to face Mom's wrath yet?

"I'm not a child anymore, Mom. Don't you think I should be able to decide what's okay?"

"The church would say otherwise. If your father hears . . ."

"You can't tell him," I cry out, startling both Mom and Sarah. I've betrayed Dad enough with the *Phantom* screening. He was finally starting to trust me. I can't even imagine how he'd feel if he heard what I'd done this afternoon.

Mom's eyes lock on me. "You know about this?"

Sarah shakes her head behind Mom's back. I'm thrown off because how could I not know about the kiss? "I . . ."

Mom whips her head to Sarah. "You told your brother what you're doing? What kind of example is that, Sarah? It's a sin!"

My mouth drops open. "Wait. You're doing . . . what?"

Sarah interjects, "He knows about *Anthony*, Mom. You're the one who's corrupting him, putting ideas into his head—"

"Shut up," Mom snaps. "Shut up. Shut up!" *Shut up* is absolutely on the forbidden phrases list, so to hear it slip from my mother's own lips is really something. We both seal our mouths and wait for whatever Mom says next. She continues in a quieter but still furious tone: "And you dared sneak him into this house, when your father and I were right there." She gestures toward her bedroom.

Sarah bites back, "So if someone I love comes to visit, it's the scandal of the century, but Calvin can have sleepovers with his little boyfriend like every other night?"

"Excuse me?" Mom whips around to face me.

Sarah tries to overpower her with a "Nothing! Never mind!"

Mom's volume rises again. "What does she mean, *boyfriend*?" The word carries so much anger and disgust.

Sure, she heard him at the window, but I didn't know Sarah knew Blake stayed over. "He's not my boyfriend!"

"*Who* isn't?"

I slap my hand over my mouth, because I've admitted that somebody slept over without permission, boyfriend or not.

"It's Blake," she guesses. "Isn't it? We warned you about him, Calvin. And you promised us it was nothing. You said he was helping you. Helping you what? Break my heart?"

I say nothing. The room is spinning. I clutch the armrest of the couch to keep from collapsing.

Mom steps around me as if I'm a piece of furniture in her way. "Does Maia know? Does her mother? This is so much worse than the fire. I can't with you. I really can't, Calvin." She exits the room, taking along any hope that this will all be okay.

Breathe. Be not afraid. Breathe.

A hand touches the top of my head, running through my hair. My eyes pop open, and Sarah is literally inches from my face. Her eyes are filling with tears that she refuses to let spill. "I'm sorry, Cal. It slipped out. I'll tell Mom I lied in the moment—"

"I kissed him," I say so softly I don't even know if she's heard.

She goes totally still, and one of her tears escapes, weaving down her cheek. It's all she needs to say. I've officially broken the toughest person I know. I sniff to hold in the small storm brewing within my own eyes. Her hand is gripping the back of my head, so I can't even look away. Slowly, her lips curl into a smile. "OMG, Calvin. That's fantastic."

I'm not even sure I've heard her correctly. "Are you making fun of me?"

"No! Listen. You haven't done anything wrong. I think it's very cool that you got to kiss someone you like."

I start blubbering at this unexpected turn. "Anthony was like the only one who took my film seriously," I tell my sister, which I hope she knows means he's okay with me. "But he could probably wash his work shirt more often."

Sarah cackles, and I can't help but grin along with her.

The joy is interrupted by Mom's voice behind me: "Get in the car."

My sister and I both stop smiling. This can't be good.

CHAPTER 33

The car rolls to a stop in front of the church. Sarah throws her head back. "Mom, I am not having this conversation with a priest."

"Maybe you should have considered that before you did what you did." She can't even bring herself to repeat what my sister did for fear that God will strike us down with lightning if we mention it in front of His own home. "Both of you," Mom adds, glancing at me in the rearview mirror. "Come on," she says, throwing off her seat belt and sliding out the door. It slams behind her.

Neither Sarah nor I budge from our seats. "If she'd left the keys, we'd be outta here so fast," she swears. We both chuckle, but can you imagine how dead we'd be then? "This is BS. I'm sorry, Cal." She unbuckles and turns to face me. "Don't tell him anything. Okay?"

I nod and unstrap my seat belt.

We both exit to find Mom with her arms crossed, impatiently waiting. The church door opens, and Father Paul emerges, a serious expression on his face. I guess for emergencies like this, the priest doesn't wait for you to come to his office. He greets you outside. I'm a little surprised he doesn't handcuff us and read us our Biblical rights.

"Let's go inside, kids," he suggests as if we have a choice.

"I'll be in the car," Mom says.

Father Paul nods and holds the door open for my sister and me. We shuffle into the church lobby and down the hall toward his office.

"Hold up," the priest says, stopping us in our tracks. We turn around to face him, and he tips his neck toward the chapel. "In here." Oh. So this chat is happening in front of Jesus too. Great.

Somehow the stained-glass lighting feels less magical this time and more like a shameful reminder of what I did. Just like the portrait at home, the sculpted Jesus refuses to look at me.

In the back corner of the church, there are three, narrow side-by-side doors: the confessionals. Father Paul leads us to the doors and says, "Pick a side, any side," as he opens the middle door for himself.

"Remember," Sarah leans in and whispers, "you didn't do anything wrong. Understand?"

I nod, but I don't understand, because I've done *everything* wrong since I fell off the stage. If I'm really honest, I'm not so sure I did much right before then either.

After a reassuring hair ruffle, Sarah takes the door to the left, and I take the one on the right. The door makes a horrible creak as it opens, and another as I close it behind me.

The confessional can't be much bigger than a coffin and is about as cheery as one. I don't remember this vibe from last time I was here. Can they change the mood based on the severity of your sins?

I kneel on a cushion facing a wicker wall. The priest has a cabinet door on the other side that he'll open when he's ready to talk to me. It's supposed to make confessing your sins anonymous when the whole congregation does it, but it doesn't really hide the shame when you've got a special one-on-one invitation from the big guy himself.

Sarah is in a matching room on the other side of Father Paul. The door on my side stays closed, so I guess he chose to open Sarah's first.

It gives me a chance to think about my sins and where I should even begin. Kissing Blake? Having him stay over? Sneaking out for the movie? Hiding the secret from my parents? Stealing the solo from Maia and lying to her about it? Dancing with Jonah? Ruining a school show? Scaring Kennedy away? I keep going further back in time, thinking of one more sin to add to the pile. When did I become the bad guy?

My mind flashes to the moment the Phantom put his arm around me and said I was the best. I know he's technically an actor, but a villain with complicated romantic feelings saying I'm the best during a trip that involved a forbidden rainbow parade that I lied about isn't necessarily the most reliable endorsement.

The cabinet door on my side slides open, and patches of light pierce through the wicker wall. It seems Father Paul's stall is much brighter than mine. I guess that makes sense, having the Lord's light surrounding him and all, while we sinners are better suited to the dark.

Father Paul clears his throat, and I realize I'm supposed to start.

There's a little speech we had to memorize in second grade that I've recited every year for my annual confessions. I guess it's required for emergency sessions too. "Bless me, Father, for I have sinned. It has been"—I do some quick math in my head—"five months since my last confession."

I can tell he's nodding. "And your sins are?"

"Not that bad, really," I say, remembering what Sarah told me and wishing I really believed it.

"I think that's for me to decide," the priest says.

"Isn't it for God to decide?"

"God is running out of patience. Now tell me what your sins are," Father Paul says with a sigh.

"Well, I ruined a school musical, and I'm going to ruin the summer solo too."

"On purpose?"

"Obviously not, but you should give the solo to Maia."

"Calvin," he warns.

"I thought this confession thing was supposed to be anonymous."

He stops, unsure what to say, until he settles on a cautionary "Young man."

"Here's the thing, Father Paul," I reply, since only my side is supposed to be anonymous. "My sins aren't mine to share. Because if I say something, someone else will get in trouble." I think of Blake and his parents. His dad practically begged me to behave. Last time we didn't, Blake got punished for a whole week. "I don't want to hurt anyone else. But you can know that I am sorry, and I'm trying to be better, and the song you shared is helping, even though I do think Maia has a better voice than me. It'd really mean the world to her to get the solo."

He grunts.

"And if you really won't change your mind, I'll do the solo like you say because I know you're the boss, or at least you're working for the Boss, and I'll keep doing the community service even though Jonah's still mad at me, and I'll keep working to be better and maybe one day, the things I've done won't seem so bad because I'll have done enough good that people will see me and not only think about the time I fell off the stage or set the priest on fire or ki—" I quickly backtrack. "Or killed every one of my friendships by being selfish. You know?"

Father Paul doesn't say anything. I press my nose against the wicker, trying to peer through and see if he's still in there. He finally says, "I know."

"Thank you for your time," I say, rising to my feet and exiting the little stall before he can assign me a series of prayers to say as penance. I expect him to burst out and tackle me, or at least to yell at me, but he stays still and silent, allowing me to escape.

I find Sarah kneeling in one of the pews pretending to pray.

"Ready?" I ask.

She nods. "So ready."

She looks miserable, but somehow, I think this has helped me. I feel almost okay.

We find Mom in the car, listening to news radio. Sarah and I climb in and buckle up.

"Well?" Mom says.

"It's between us and God," Sarah says with so much smugness I kind of love it. She's got Mom there.

Mom frowns as she puts the car into drive. "And this"—she takes one hand off the wheel to make a little circle with her finger—"is between the three of us."

"You mean you're not going to tell Dad?" I pipe up from the back seat.

"And ruin his perfect image of you kids?"

Sarah snorts, and even I have to wonder if it's *our* image that Mom's most worried about. The last time Mom outsourced our punishments, Dad was so mad I thought they were going to split up right in the parking lot. Is Mom really protecting Dad, us, or herself?

I can't decide whether to be relieved or whether I should send my mother directly to Father Paul to confess about lying to her husband. Dad deserves to know what a mess I've made, but I can't bear the thought of this family falling further apart because of me. We're not like Maia's family. We're too fragile to handle all the mess I'm bringing into our lives.

"I won't tell him," I promise, zipping my lips closed for the rest of the ride.

CHAPTER 34

After a silent dinner, I excuse myself to my room because I'm awfully tired—wink, wink. I'm actually grounded but don't tell Dad. Mom's got Sarah's and my phones and computers tucked away in her closet somewhere, so I can't even tell my friends, assuming I have any left.

I open the blinds and stare into the darkness with a stomach unsettled by the guilt of letting my parents down. With the bedroom lights flipped off, I can see the backyard clearly. I wait for Blake, because how can he not come find me after everything that happened today?

Shortly after nine, a figure emerges from the shadows. The invisible spiders start twitching inside. When he's almost reached the window, I can make out his nervous smile, which stretches wider when our eyes meet. That smile sends me floating toward the ceiling, but the memory of confession quickly drops me back onto the floor, ready to do what needs to be done.

Today's kiss can't mean anything and can never happen again. I can't risk hurting my parents, or him, or anyone else.

"Open up," I hear him say through the glass.

I shake my head. "I can't."

"It's easy," he says. He pantomimes unlocking and raising a window, then pokes his head through the invisible opening. His hands prop up his chin with his hands, resting his elbows on the imaginary windowsill. It's adorable, and he said he wasn't an actor. Jonah's reminder that Blake is the new Kennedy somehow feels even truer.

"You have to go."

"Is this about the ki—"

"Stop," I nearly shout, because what if my parents hear? "It was just a movie. And we have to pretend it never happened."

"But it did happen. And it wasn't just a movie."

"My mom knows you slept over. And my dad . . ." A sob spills out. I sniff up the snot and try again. "The other night, after we saw *Phantom*, he—he told me God has a plan for me." I can barely see him through the blur of my tears. "And that plan isn't you."

"He said that?" Blake's mouth drops open. "Let me in, and we can talk about it."

"I don't want to talk about it," I lie. "I don't need you to come in and fix me. I am not broken." I use Jonah's words because I can't think of my own. "I don't need another Kennedy."

"I am nothing like Kennedy!" he protests.

"You're right," I admit. "She could see I wasn't worth it. Please be more like her now and go away. Don't visit. Don't text me."

Silent tears wiggle down Blake's cheek. I want to hold his hand so badly, and not even as a friend, which is how I know I need to close the blinds. I reach for the little string.

"Goodbye, Blake," I say in a broken voice. The blinds unfurl before I have to see his reaction.

I let out a sniffling, sobbing, grumbling groan that I hope he can't hear through the window. I flop onto the bed and cry myself to sleep.

The next week, it's just me, Sarah, and Mom at home all day, every day. At first, Sarah wants to talk about my secret, but after the fifth or sixth "Leave me alone," she finally gets the hint. Mom doesn't try to talk about what she thinks happened at all, which is surprising but fine with me.

I spend my days practicing for the church solo, because that's what I promised Father Paul I would do. I'm only allowed to leave the house for rehearsals and, of course, church. Maia does not show up for either rehearsal. It seems she quit choir after not getting the solo, which honestly isn't the Jesusly thing to do, but I understand.

When Mom's Bible Study meets on Tuesday, she parades me around in front of them so they can all see how perfectly normal I am. Mrs. Ruiz isn't there, but Mrs. Brunelle notes how much I've grown this summer. I smile although somehow, I feel smaller than ever.

That evening, there's another tap on the window. I grab the string and yank the blinds open, unsure if I want to hug Blake or scream at him to leave, but desperate to see him either way. I don't have to decide because he's already running away.

My chest feels as empty as the yard.

I'm about to close the blinds when I notice something small taped on the outside of the screen. I crack open the window and the screen to grab it. It's a flash drive.

I sneak into Dad's home office. The walls are covered with baseball posters, like mine, but his are framed and "vintage," some of them even signed. They seem naked without *Phantom* masks if you ask me, but nobody does. I creep over to the desk, open the General's laptop, and plug in the USB. A single file appears. I open it with a click.

A movie begins. Our movie.

Typed credits play over a recording of Maia's singing.

CALVIN CONROY PRESENTS
MANHATTAN MELODY

The credits are followed by the opening scene: Maia in a semiformal gown, clutching four trophies to her chest. Sarah, Michal, Anthony, and I face her, seated in folding chairs and dressed as reporters. "Melody Monarchy, Melody Monarchy, over here," Anthony says in a thick New York accent that still makes me laugh. "How does it feel to be the first person to win all four awards of the coveted EGOT in a single night?"

"These ole things." Maia blushes. "Truly magical."

The scene continues. As Melody Monarchy pauses to think back on her small-town life, Blake has added a rewind sound that makes our backwards movements even funnier than I could have imagined. A smile spreads across my face. Blake edited the movie. I don't know why he would bother after the things I said to him, but he did, and it's perfect.

I hit Pause, because Kennedy needs to see this now. Really, she needed to see it like a month ago, but maybe it's not too late.

I open my email account, address a new message to Kennedy, and attach the file. I throw a purple heart into the subject line and an I hope this explains everything in the body. Send.

I close my email and go back to the movie. Right before I can hit Play, Mom appears in the doorway. "What are you doing in here?" she demands.

I somehow manage to close the file before she can see, but she immediately strides over and snatches my Dad's laptop. "I don't think so." Without another word, the computer and my movie are gone.

That night, I wait for Blake to return so I can thank him for the movie, but he doesn't come back.

The days crawl along, and finally, Mom ceremoniously hands me back my phone.

As it powers on, I wait for the notices of missed messages from my friends to come piling in, but there's not a single notification. No call or text or anything.

I guess I shouldn't be surprised, but that doesn't mean I'm not sad too.

"Get your suit out," Mom says.

"My suit?" I ask. "The church solo isn't until tomorrow."

"What are you talking about?" She dives into my closet herself and pulls out the hanging plastic bag containing my fanciest outfit. "It's Jonah's bar mitzvah."

My eyes widen. That's today? I completely lost track of the date. "Oh, I don't think he wants me there."

"Don't be ridiculous. You said yes months ago, and he's your best friend." She unzips the bag and pulls out the jacket and slacks. Heading back to my closet to retrieve a button-down shirt, she adds, "Besides, Kennedy will be there."

Honestly, I forgot she'd even be in town for this, which means she is in town right now and she hasn't texted me either. I open Instagram on my newly returned phone and pull up Kennedy's page. Still blocked. My knees cave and I plop on top of my unmade bed. "I'm not feeling great." It's true. It hurts too much to know that my friends officially hate me.

She places a hand on my forehead and keeps it there for five seconds before commanding, "Get dressed. Unless you'd like me to change you?"

"Okay, fine. I'll do it. Just go." I gather up my suit in my arms.

Mom sighs as she heads toward the door. "I really don't understand what happened between you and your friends, Calvin." Her eyes turn toward the window, and I know she's picturing Blake. "But I miss my sweet boy."

She closes the door behind her. I wonder where her sweet boy went, and if it's too late to run away with him and save myself from whatever comes next.

CHAPTER 35

Mom drops me off at the front door of the temple. For once, I kind of wish she was staying with me, but she wasn't invited. I'm on my own. I have no idea what to expect and no friends to lean on.

When I step inside, I'm greeted by a friendly woman with dark skin and silver hair, about my grandma's age. Her dress is speckled with yellow flowers. She's holding a basket full of little caps and beckons for me to take one. "Kippah, sweetie?" she offers.

I take a shiny green cap and place it on top of my head. It seems to stay well enough, but I'm afraid I'll lose it as I walk away. As if reading my mind, she reaches into a glass jar by her side and extracts a pair of bobby pins. Hat secured, I follow her gesture into the next set of open doors.

My mouth drops open as I take in the room. Rows of chairs face a stage-like area. A fancy cabinet rests in the middle. Tall, multi-armed candleholders stand proudly on either side. In front sits a small table and podium. The space looks a lot like a church, but also not. It's both comforting and dizzying.

I walk down the rows of seats, looking for a place safely in the middle where nobody will see me. I don't recognize many of these people, and I realize that I've never met Jonah's extended family before. About half the guests are Black. I haven't seen a person outside my immediate family in a week, but somehow, I feel more alone in this crowd of Jonah's loved ones than I did locked away in my bedroom. I guess I'm used to being around mostly white people, and I hadn't given it much thought before. I wonder if this is how Jonah and Maia feel in school. Maia's comment replays in my head, and I realize she may be right. I have some work to do if I ever want to be a better friend.

I slide into a row beside a woman wearing a navy dress. Her hair is curled just so. She smiles at me with bright pink lips that pop against her warm umber skin. I smile back as I settle down.

I spot Kennedy on the opposite side of the room.

She's sitting next to . . . Maia? Maia sees me and waves. It almost looks like she's gesturing me to join them, but I'm sure I've misunderstood. Kennedy whispers something in her ear, and they both chuckle. At least our film brought *somebody* closer together. I don't have much time to dwell on this new alliance, as the woman beside me taps me on the knee.

"How do you know the man of honor, hon?" she asks with the sort of hushed whisper we'd use in church.

She sounds so sweet that I instantly know I chose the right seat. "I'm his best—" I realize after everything that's happened, this word might be a serious overstatement, and I quickly backtrack. "I'm his friend."

"Well, I'm his favorite . . ." She pauses to give me a dramatic wink. "I'm his aunt."

Is this his dad's sister? Aunt Dorothy, who bought us the theater tickets? I didn't know Jonah's dad very well, but I've heard so much about him. Being beside someone so close to him, I can't help but smile. "I think I know who you are," I say. "And I'm so happy you're here for him."

"Well, aren't you the sweetest."

Before I can correct her, the service begins.

I catch Jonah in the front row with a white embroidered shawl draped over his shoulder. He's wearing his dad's necktie. His kippah covers the top of his curls. It's not something he normally wears, and for some reason all I can think about is those drama maidens swooning. His mom sits on one side of him and Michal on the other, both sporting new hairstyles. So much has changed in the past week.

As the rabbi leads the room in prayers, I do my best to follow along in the prayer book, sitting and standing with the crowd and silently moving my lips as they speak. Members of Jonah's family and even our community service buddies take turns praying aloud at the front.

Nothing is as hypnotizing as when Jonah reads from the giant scroll in Hebrew. I'm on the edge of my seat, and I can't help but wonder what he's saying. I can barely speak in front of a crowd without making a scene, but here he is, gliding over the words like a verbal figure skater. His voice shakes with emotion as he reads certain phrases, and I realize he's not just saying the words. He's *feeling* them. Even though I don't understand the language, I start feeling them too.

Jonah's eyes are turned down, following the silver pointer in his hand as it traces the text and keeps his place, but I know he has the whole thing memorized. The concentration and passion seem so natural. I think about the song Father Paul is making me sing (tomorrow!!!) and I can't imagine being so moved by the words. This is something else. This is what my parents wish I would feel in church. What is it that's moving him so much? What am I missing? I realize, as I listen to this scripture reading and to Jonah's speech afterward, that there is so much about Jonah that I don't know.

Jonah's mom approaches the front next. "Jonah, we are so proud of you and the young man you've become." She wipes a tear from her eye. Everyone there knows exactly who she means by "we." There's a long pause as she attempts to regain her composure. Jonah was right when he said today was going to be difficult for her too. I hope the dance helps.

"Every day, I see more of your father in you. Today more than ever. I could truly feel his faith in your words, his joy in your smile, his passion in your tears. But no more tears. Not today." She sniffs, trying to follow her own advice. "Today we celebrate my sweet, brave boy who defied so many obstacles to become the man we see before us. Today, Jonah, we celebrate you."

A silent tear escapes and trickles down my face, and more follow. Jonah's aunt rummages through her purse before extracting a tissue. She leans over and hands it me.

Thank you, I mouth, dabbing my cheek.

After the service ends, Aunt Dorothy leans over once more and says, "I think I know who you are too. And the way he talks about you, I think it's safe to say *best*."

I can't help but grin when I hear this, even if it's no longer true.

CHAPTER 36

A crowd gathers to congratulate Jonah. I don't think he needs to see me right now, so instead I shuffle out the door toward the shuttle buses that will take us to the reception at the Marriott across town. I see Maia and Kennedy get onto the front bus, so I board the second.

The seats and floor are lined with a scratchy gray carpet decorated with scattered rainbow streaks. I remember the last time I was on a bus, the last day of school, when I befriended Blake and found out that Kennedy was moving. How things have changed.

"Say, Calvin!" Amos says, waving at me. His wheelchair is buckled to the floor across from the middle exit door. Charles has taken a seat in the row directly behind him. "Sit with us!"

I have nowhere else to go, and it's nice to see some familiar faces that don't hate me, so I settle down beside Charles.

"Lovely ceremony," Charles says.

"So beautiful," I agree.

"We missed you this week. I'm glad you could be here for Jonah. I know it means a lot to him."

I want to admit that I've actually failed Jonah in so many ways, but I bite my tongue. Instead I listen to them reminisce about their own bar mitzvahs. The whole bumpy ride, my mind rattles and reminds me that I don't belong here.

When the bus comes to a stop, I take my time getting off, not sure what to expect for the next part of the day. The bus driver comes over to help Amos exit with his chair, and I realize I'm just in the way. I reluctantly say goodbye to the pair and follow the crowd.

Inside, I find myself in a ballroom half the size of the school gym. Round tables circle the perimeter. A DJ is set up at the edge of a dance floor, neon lights shooting from his table and illuminating the ceiling. It reminds me of my cousin's wedding.

I notice Jonah's aunt push through the crowd and head toward the sole rectangular table, located directly across from the DJ. There are tons of empty seats there.

I race toward that space but am stopped by an older gentleman who tsks at me and says, "Place cards." He points to a small round table by the door that I somehow overlooked. I wander over and find a series of adorable tiny Playbills, each featuring the name of a guest and a table number. I scoop up the little Playbill with my name on the cover, which is honestly a dream come true in itself. *Calvin Conroy: Table 6.*

As I scan the reception hall for my table, I wonder what that show would be about. Once I spot my actual seat, my heart sinks. Maia and Kennedy are there, sitting side by side. Looks like *Calvin Conroy: Table 6* is a melodrama.

I slink toward my spot and pull out the chair beside Kennedy. Might as well face this head-on. Other kids from the school play fill in the seats around us.

"Hey, Calvin," Maia says in a tone that feels genuinely nice and catches me off guard.

"You're looking well," I say to both of them.

"Very well indeed," Kennedy replies in a pretend-snooty voice, fluffing her hair.

We laugh. Maybe this won't be so bad after all. I slip off my blazer and drape it across the back of my chair before taking a seat.

"It was a typo," I softly say to Kennedy, unable to meet her eyes.

"Okay," she says sadly. I can't tell if she believes me or not. "I liked your movie."

My lips curl into a smile. "You watched it?"

She nods.

"Keeping it a surprise all summer was so hard. And maybe not the best idea. I didn't mean to push you away."

"We both did a little pushing," she admits.

That's as far as we get before a voice blasts, "Good afternoon, my frieeeeeeennnnnnds!" I'm closest to the DJ, which means I jump the highest as he screams into the microphone behind me to get the crowd pumping. "Welcome to the moment we've been waiting thirteen years for."

The sound of dozens of chairs pushing back fills the room as everyone stands. I quickly get to my feet. The music picks up a bouncy vibe, and the adults begin bopping and clapping along.

"Escorted by his mother, Marian, and sister, Michal, I present to you the bar mitzvah, Jonah Franklin."

The crowd goes wild as Jonah enters the room, his mother on one side, Michal on the other. He shimmies and sways to the music, his swoopy curls fluttering with the motion. All of the drama maidens at our table are swooning. It is pretty cute. He raises his right hand and lets Michal do a fancy spin under his arm. The crowd loves it. Next, he looks at his mom, who gives him a playful *don't you dare* glare. He slowly raises his left arm. His mother is too tall for this, but the crowd is eating it up, so she gives an *oh fine* sort of eye roll, bends down, and spins beneath her son's arm.

I'm grinning so much that I almost forget for one second how much my former friend hates me. Jonah, his mom, and his sister head to the special table set aside for them, the rectangular one with his aunt Dorothy. I'm relieved that I didn't make the ultimate faux pas and accidentally take Jonah's seat.

A series of servers emerge from the swinging kitchen doors, carrying plates of delicious-smelling foods.

"Pasta or chicken?" one asks me as she settles a tray carrying some of each onto a folding tray stand.

"Chicken, please," I say, though I'm hungry enough that I almost want to ask for one of each. Right as the plate is placed before me, there's a "May

I have your attention, please!" from the microphone that makes me jump. The server flinches.

Aunt Dorothy is standing by the DJ table, and she has a few words to say. She talks about the shows she and Jonah have seen together and the songs they've belted out on their long yearly drive to the Cape (hers quite off-key, though Jonah was much too sweet to say so). She wraps up with "Your father would be proud, Jonah, and I should know. That man was the biggest pain in my side, so nobody was closer to him than me." Everyone is laugh-crying now. "Mazel tov!" The adults raise their glasses. I clap.

I've taken a few bites of my chicken when another voice says, "I'd like to say something too." I again turn and see Charles holding up the mic. "Because this young man changed my life. And I know you're all saying it's a little late for this old guy's life to be changed, but I'm here to tell you that you're wrong. When my husband and I first met Jonah and his friend at the retirement community, we knew we were in for a ride."

Wait. Husband?

Amos and Charles are married? I can't believe I thought they were just card partners. I try to remember what Jonah said about wanting what they have one day. Did he know? Yeesh, of course he did. My face burns, though I'm not sure why I'm embarrassed. I haven't stumbled upon a shameful secret. I'm just catching up to what's been true all along, and for once, I actually *am* perfectly fine with it.

I listen to Charles's tear-inducing speech about a series of things Jonah did at community service that I somehow completely missed.

More applause and drinks raised to the sky.

"Right on!" the DJ says. "Let's keep the love going, friends. If you're a Jonah fan, come on up and tell us!"

Suddenly my heart sinks. Is *everybody* supposed to make a speech? I'm obviously a huge Jonah fan. The biggest. But how am I supposed to make a speech? Won't that upset him?

One of Jonah's uncles starts talking now, but I hardly hear what he says. When he's done, he rests the microphone on the table beside the DJ. My stomach twists as I wonder who will go next. If it's Kennedy, will she steal the material that I would want to say so my jokes are less funny? Is the crowd expecting funny? I'm not sure I could even go for understandable at this point. Why didn't Jonah tell me about the speaking?

Breathe, Blake whispers in my mind, which is exactly what I do. I push my chair back too forcefully. It loudly scrapes against the floor as I stand. Everyone's definitely looking at me now, so there's no backing out. I take a few steps forward, grateful that my table is right next to the DJ's. My arm reaches out. My fingers curl around the cold metal of the microphone, and my thumb pushes the bumpy plastic On button.

"Hello, everyone," I say, cringing at the sound of my voice amplified for all to hear. No wonder Miss H. didn't give me a microphone reserved for the leads. I lock eyes with Jonah, sitting at the head table. His unreadable brown eyes flicker in the candlelight from his table's centerpiece. "I'm Calvin, Jonah's best friend." He doesn't seem to cringe, so maybe there's hope for us still.

With a dash of regret that my blazer is on the back of the chair and not covering my growing pit stains, I continue. "I want to thank everyone for being here today for Jonah. I'm not Jewish, so I admit I didn't know what to expect. But the amount of love and support in this room is overwhelming and beautiful. I feel so lucky to be able to witness this. To be Jonah right now, wow, I cannot even imagine. You are so loved my friend." I have to sniff deeply before I can get out, "Like, you have no idea." I hope he knows what I'm talking about.

His head bobs up and down, so I think I'm doing okay.

"And I messed up this summer." My eyes coast over to Maia and Kennedy. "I messed up a lot, actually." Maia nods in agreement. "But Jonah, through it all, you always saw the best in me, and that made me want to be a better version of myself. A better friend. A better *person*. Like, look at me now. I'm talking in front of a room of strangers, and I haven't fallen down or set the room on fire yet." Everyone laughs. "And even if I did fall, I know you'd be there to catch me. Like you always are. I hope one day I can do the same for you. So anyway, that's about it, I guess, so I'll say thank you, and sorry, and thank you again. And, what's that word?"

"Mazel tov," Maia calls.

"Mazel tov!" I call out, as everyone joins me. The old me would love this moment, the attention and the applause.

But this is Jonah's day, not mine. I extend my arm, holding the microphone out to the crowd. "Who's next?"

I scan the room, but nobody makes a move.

My dripping eyes widen as I realize I might have made a horrible mistake.

"I am so, so sorry," I say again, before tossing the microphone onto the table behind me and racing out the room.

CHAPTER 37

I can't believe I did that. I've ruined an entire bar mitzvah celebration. I made this beautiful day all about me. And it's not. It's really not. I'll text Jonah tomorrow and maybe he'll forgive me. For now, I'm calling Mom and telling her to get me out of here.

I slap my pants pockets before realizing my phone is tucked away in my coat pocket, and my coat is slung over my chair back in the ballroom. I wonder how long it would take to walk home from here, or if I'd even know the way.

I push into the bathroom. I don't have to pee, but I can hide here until everyone has forgotten about me, then slip in, grab my suit jacket, and make my escape. My nose is greeted by the scent of oranges, which is not so bad, considering where I am. The room is a tribute to the color *cream*, with tiles in various shades of tan lining the off-white floor and walls.

As I'm wondering whether it might be safer to wait inside a stall, the door swings open.

It's Jonah.

So, this is happening now.

"Hey," I say to him.

He nods back. "Hey."

"I thought everyone had to make a speech," I try to explain. "It was silly. I'm ridiculous."

He shakes his head. "It wasn't silly. It was nice." The redness surrounding his pupils begs to differ, but it's a kind sentiment.

We stand there facing each other but not saying a word. I take in his suit up close for the first time. There are flecks of white and black that pop from the sturdy gray fabric. His kippah is a dark blue, which looks great with the light blue shirt and his dad's tie.

I wonder how long this stare-down will last before somebody realizes that Jonah is missing from his own bar mitzvah celebration and comes in here to rescue him. And here I am, keeping him from everyone he loves. "Okay, I should probably let you go, though," I say.

"Of course," he says with a snort. "You tend to do that."

"Do what?"

"Stop me whenever I'm feeling almost brave enough to tell you something."

"Come on, Jonah," I laugh, patting his arm. "Did you see yourself today? You're the bravest person I know."

"Then how come you fell for Blake?"

"I . . . what?" This is not a talk I expected to have today. Or ever. I promised myself that the things I thought I was thinking were not real, and for my parents' sake, I have to believe that. "I . . ." I try to protest, but he holds up a finger and brings it to his lips.

"You got your speech," he says. "Give me mine. Before I drop the mic and run from the room screaming."

I laugh, but my heart is thumping even louder now than it did during my toast.

He clears his throat. "Okay, a few things." He holds up one finger. "One. You've been beating yourself up about supposedly ruining the play, but you didn't ruin anything. You were funny and sweet and trying really hard. I was the prince, but *you* were charming. The moment you fell into my arms with that slipper was my favorite part of the whole production."

I'm brought back to that moment, my knees feeling weak, my back pressed against his chest. I remember the way he told me it was going to be okay. I felt so safe.

He holds up his second finger. "Two. Blake thinks he can edit you. Crop the scene. Change the star. But you don't need to be edited. You don't need to be fixed. That was my most perfect moment on stage."

Don't cry. Don't cry. Don't cry.

"Because three"—the third finger comes up— "it made me feel something." It's a very loaded *something*. "I was wrong earlier. You're not perfect, Calvin. You're messy and funny and emotional and real and sometimes you set people on fire. Sometimes you fall off the stage. But you always get up again. You never give up. And that's so much better than perfect to me."

Crying. Crying. Crying.

"I never meant to push you away when you fell off the stage, but I needed a minute to . . . to understand and accept what I was feeling. It was new to me. But I know now. So, when you and Blake shared that kiss, the kiss that I wanted all summer . . ."

"You're not making any sense," I stammer, even though my twisting stomach understands perfectly. "You told me you used to have a crush on Ken—"

"I did. I used to. I guess I'm bi," he says, "Or maybe pan, or . . . well, I'm figuring it out. But I know exactly how I feel about you, Cal. Can I . . . ?"

Without thinking about it—which is weird because up until now I've been thinking nonstop—I nod.

He leans forward and kisses me on the lips. It lasts all of two seconds. When he pulls away, my face follows his and I go in for another. This one lasts an extra second or two, giving me time to taste the pasta sauce on his breath. I almost regret choosing the chicken.

My stomach is a fruit salad of emotions. I'm shocked because I didn't expect it. Nervous because what if my parents find out? Guilty because Blake kissed me first. Confused by how much I want to try it again. "Jonah, I just kissed *another* boy," I whisper as if he wasn't my co-kisser.

"Actually," Jonah says with a smugness I'd expect from Kennedy, "it's my bar mitzvah. You just kissed a *man*."

We both cackle, and our lips meet as the bathroom door swings open.

We step back but are not quick enough.

"What in the actual—"

"Kennedy!" I cry out.

"So it *wasn't* a typo," she says, glaring at me.

The hairs on my cheek prickle.

In a mocking lovesick voice, she goes on, "*Things are things with Jonah. But things are things with someone else too.*"

My knees buckle. I grab the countertop to keep myself from falling onto the floor.

"Will you get out of here?" Jonah yells, and for one second, I think he means me. He was never supposed to know exactly what I said. I was never supposed to say it. "NOW, Kennedy," he adds.

She spins and exits. The door swings closed behind her.

We both stand in awkward silence, staring at the door, until his phone buzzes. He pulls it out, and his mouth drops open.

"She posted it," he says.

"Who posted what?" I ask.

"I guess Kennedy unblocked us, and . . . she posted the kiss."

"Kiss?" I can feel my face redden. "Was she film-ing us?" I scan the bathroom, looking for the hidden camera.

"No," he says, sounding exasperated. "The one with Blake. Someone must've sent her the movie."

I yank the phone from his hands. Blake and I kiss in slow motion in the little video on Jonah's screen. Despite some decent editing, it's clear to all (I glance at the number of likes) thirteen Kennedians exactly who it is that I'm kissing. For once, I am glad my parents don't allow her to tag me on her page and that she actually respected their wishes.

The caption reads, *When your friend waits until you leave to get interesting . . .*

"How could she do this?" Jonah asks.

"I have to call Blake," I say, worried for him.

"I'll get her to delete it," Jonah tells me before storming out of the bathroom, though I honestly can't tell if he's more jealous of Blake than upset that my whole life is ruined.

Falling off the stage has nothing on this.

CHAPTER 38

I dart toward the reception hall to grab my phone. The space has darkened and is thumping with the sound of music. Maia tries to grab my attention, but as soon as I've snatched up my jacket, I make a break for the freedom of the outdoors.

I dial Blake's number but he doesn't answer.

A rideshare car drives past and rolls to a stop in the driveway. I look back toward the building's entrance and see Kennedy come through the revolving door. She spots me but makes a wide circle to avoid me as she heads toward the car.

I race toward her, unsure where to even begin but knowing I can't just let this go. "Kennedy!"

"I deleted it," she whispers, eyes turned down to the pavement.

I think she expects me to melt and thank her, but

I'm so furious and overwhelmed that I shout, "Why did you even post it?"

"You lied to me! I thought Jonah liked . . ." Her jaw quivers.

"I didn't know he liked me either. I didn't know this was going to happen," I say, defending myself even though I don't think I have to. It only took her a second to post that specific clip, which means she had it cut and ready to go. She was waiting. "Did you think for one second how posting that would make me feel?"

"Jeez, Cal. It was up for like two seconds. I said I deleted it."

"That's not good enough!" My arms flail. "What if Sarah saw? Or anyone at church? Did they?"

"How would I know?"

"You mean *why would you care*? You were my best friend, Kennedy, but I see now that to you, I was just your biggest fan."

Her shoulders slump. "Was?"

Of course that's what she got from my dramatic pronouncement. I take a breath. "I'm done letting you distract me from the people who, for some messed-up reason, might actually care about me."

"I . . ." Kennedy trails off. "Okay, fine." With

a deep inhale, she reminds me of myself, pre-live performance, terrified of everything that can (and knowing me, will) go wrong. She even forgets to use her project-for-the-folks-in-the-back voice when she says, "FYI, I applied to the school in New York long before you fell off the stage."

Wait. So she lied about that, just to hurt me? I should be mad or sad or . . . something, but I think I'm at capacity for all those emotions.

"I know," I fib. "You're a good actress, but you're not that good."

Kennedy's mouth drops open.

I cross the valet driveway and am heading toward the street when I hear someone calling my name. Maia catches up to me at the curb. "Calvin—"

"If this is about the solo tomorrow—" I begin.

"Calvin—"

"You were right," I say.

"About which part?" she asks even though we both know she was right about everything.

"You deserved that solo," I tell her. Because she did. She really did. "It was like the one thing you wanted all summer, and I stole it. I thought I could convince Father Paul to give it back to you, but I still should've told you the truth. It was messed up to lie, and I understand why you hate me. I really did love hanging out with you this summer, and I hate that I messed it up. I'm so sorry. For everything."

Maia lets out a long sigh and sits on the curb. She pats the space beside her, so I take a seat.

"I would've apologized sooner," I continue, "but Mom took my phone and I haven't seen you in a while. I do wish you hadn't quit the choir. You really do have an amazing voice."

"I didn't quit," she finally says with a laugh. "My family went on vacation. I thought my mom would've told yours. And for what it's worth, the solo wasn't the only thing I cared about this summer." She sighs again. "It's funny. Until it all fell apart, I had the best summer of my life."

"That's not funny," I say. "It's sad." Which is so rude that I quickly cover my mouth. "I mean, I'm happy for you? I mean—"

"Shut up, Calvin." She laughs. "It is sad." She bumps her shoulder into mine. "Real smooth, by the way. Replacing me with your dream man in the movie."

My face flushes. "Blake is not my dream man," I say a little too forcefully. "It was Blake's idea. Besides, he was the best person for the part."

"Dang. I would hate to see who else showed up for those auditions."

This makes us both laugh, until I remember the reason we're outside. That kiss was online for everyone to see, while another is fresh in my mind and on my lips.

"I can't believe Kennedy posted it," Maia says. "She's been nothing but nice to me all day. I should've known she was up to something."

I bury my face in my hands. "I kissed Jonah. She saw."

"Calvin! Look at you!" I know she's dying to break out into a chorus of *Tell me more, tell me more.*

I wish I could feel her excitement, but it's hard since my life is pretty much ruined.

"Kennedy is such a . . ." Maia freezes at the word she knows would give my parents a heart attack if I heard. "You know."

"Wicked Witch," I finish the thought for her. "Though it looked like you two were having a hoot and a half in there."

"Please," Maia *pffts*. "I only felt sorry for her after what happened to her last week. I thought she could use a friend, you know?"

What? "What happened last week?" I ask.

Maia perks up. "I forgot you were grounded."

"And blocked," I add.

She pulls out her own phone. I expect to see Blake and my kiss all over again, but instead she shows me a video of a stage. I recognize Kennedy's "new BFF" from her Instagram post, dressed as Galinda from *Wicked*. The girl by her side has a painted green face. "Is that Kennedy?"

Maia nods. "Keep watching."

I see my old friend belt and almost hit the notes that Maia would have crushed, before she picks up the broomstick to defy gravity. Except somehow, the broom gets tangled in her skirt, swipes at her ankle, and sends her face down onto the stage.

There is a THWACK that leaves me speechless.

As the fallen star tries to push herself up, the broom says *Not today* and sweeps out her other leg. She topples into the orchestra.

O.

M.

G.

Kennedy Carmichael fell off the stage.

"I . . ." I have no words.

"Everyone at NYYAPA's posting it," Maia says. "Think of all the new *fall*-owers."

It's hilarious, but for some reason I don't want to laugh along. "Too bad you weren't there to save the broom," I tell Maia instead.

"Huh?"

"Like when I fell. And you lunged for the shoe. I know your mom worked hard on it and all—"

"Calvin, you fool! I was lunging for you."

My insides flutter like I have stage fright, but a good kind. All of my friends witnessed my fall— Blake, Jonah, Maia—and they all had a reaction I never could have imagined. Somehow, the fall doesn't seem as important as the friends who helped to pick me back up again.

I smile at Maia. "Shall we?" I tip my head toward the hotel's entrance, where the party of a lifetime awaits.

CHAPTER 39

The whole ride home, I freak out as I try to decide whether Mom and Dad know I'm hiding something. Each new "So, what else did you do tonight?" feels like a leading question, designed to uncover my conversation with Jonah or the post on Kennedy's Instagram.

"They put Jonah on a chair and threw him in the air while we danced," I say instead. "It was fun." Plus beautiful, emotional, confusing, stressful, then back to fun again.

"Nice," the General says from the front seat, and I think he means it.

It seems I'm safe. For now.

When we get home, I run to my room. "Very tired," I lie to my parents, but I'm not sure I'll be able to sleep, between everything that happened today and the church solo tomorrow.

I pull out my phone. There are texts from Maia and Jonah checking in on me. Jonah adds, Today was . . . dancer emoji, flame emoji, one-hundred emoji.

I laugh, because it really was. I send them each a thumbs up and a smiley face before starting a text of my own. I need to tell Blake what Kennedy did, even though I haven't heard from him since I closed the blinds on him after we kissed.

I glance up at the posters decorating the walls of my room. Each baseball player wears a paper *Phantom* mask with pride. Hold on—am I Christine here? Torn between the mysterious stranger trying to fix me and the old friend who's been there all along, but sometimes not. A third option floats into my mind: the parents who would flip out if they knew I was having these thoughts at all.

I glance back to the unsent text to Blake on my phone. Can we talk? I stare at the message for a minute wondering what else I should even say. I can't decide, so I delete the message and slide open my window. Maybe seeing him will help.

I throw one leg outside, and then the other. With a deep breath, I slide down, crashing into the shrubs beneath. I realize a little too late that I should have perhaps changed out of my suit. I pop to my feet, swish the debris off my butt, and race over to Blake's house.

I've never been inside before, so it takes me tapping on three windows before I get the right one, but finally he shows up in the glass, looking down at me.

"Go away, Calvin," he says, but he doesn't move.

I grab onto the windowsill and try to hoist myself up. I make it about one foot off the ground, groaning and panting and kicking the siding as I try to Spider-Man climb into his room.

Blake laughs at the struggle and mercifully slides open his screen. He bends down, grips under my arms, and hoists me up. With a few grunts of his own, he drags me into his bedroom. He stumbles backward, and I flop on top of him, leaving the pair of us in a heap on the floor.

I quickly push myself up and take in his bedroom. Sharpie doodles that match his hand-drawn arm tattoos are sprinkled across one of the white walls. The bed is tightly made, and unlike in my room, there is absolutely no unwashed laundry scattered on the floor. In one corner, there's a small desk with a laptop plus a massive computer that must be ancient.

I walk up to the big monitor. "Why'd you edit the film?" I ask as I run my finger along the hunk of plastic, accidentally wiping up a trail of dust in the process.

"I said I would. And I know how much it meant to you."

"And you kept the . . . you know?" I can't say the word that I can't stop thinking about because I'm afraid I'll blush even more than I already am.

He smirks. "It's my favorite part."

"Kennedy's too," I say. "She posted it."

He blinks a couple of times. "Wow. Classy."

"It's down now. But . . . ?"

Blake shrugs. "I'm not afraid."

The church solo song flickers into my mind: "Be Not Afraid." I don't think Blake is afraid of anything, and I feel like I'm letting him down by freaking out. By pushing him away. By kissing Jonah.

"I am so afraid," I tell him.

"Okay."

"And I kissed Jonah."

There's the cringe I've been waiting for. Blake takes a breath. "And?"

"I . . . don't know." I'm surprised I can say this without crying. "Ever since you and I kissed, I've been thinking about it constantly, but my mom found out about our sleepover and made me confess to our priest, which I kind of did but not really, and then I was grounded even though my dad doesn't know and the second I was freed, it was suddenly time for Jonah's bar mitzvah and I'm making a speech, which I totally wasn't supposed to do, but I guess it was a good speech because then Jonah kissed me, and I didn't even fall as I was speaking, which is totally because of you, and completely unlike Kennedy, who fell off the stage like me by the way. Stars. They're exactly like us, you know?"

Blake shakes his head, speechless. His nostrils flare and his eyes water as he takes a seat on the edge of his bed.

I have a seat beside him and take his hand, but it's different this time. Friends may hold friends' hands all the time, but it doesn't feel the same after you've kissed two of your three remaining friends. I'm super aware of how slimy my sweat-coated palms must feel.

Thankfully, Blake pulls away from my swampy frog hands almost immediately.

"I really do like hanging out with you, Calvin," he manages to say, which is such a relief until he continues: "But enough with the mixed messages. Holding my hand. Grabbing my pinkie. Keeping my feet warm. Yeah, we didn't talk about it, but I have a hard time believing you didn't understand what any of that meant. You need to decide what you want."

As if my opinion even matters. "As soon as my parents find out about Kennedy's post, and you know they will, I'll be grounded for life, and friends will be a thing of my past."

"And who do you want to see when that punishment finally ends?"

"You don't understand," I push back, rising to my feet on shaking legs. "It's never going to end."

I wait for Blake to comfort me, to say it'll be okay, to tell me to breathe, but he doesn't. "It will someday. If nothing else, someday you'll be older and your parents won't be able to decide what you're allowed to do or who you're allowed to kiss anymore. And in the meantime, Calvin, you can still control how you treat other people. How you treat me. Do you know how it felt to finally kiss my crush, then watch him run away with some other guy, literally disappearing on me and shutting me out? I know this sucks, stinks, smells real ickalicious. But I need to know if you want to be with me, or with Jonah."

How can he ask me to choose between the old and the new? Between the one who would devastate Kennedy and the one my parents warned me about. Between the one who's told me I'm perfect and the one who makes me feel like I might be okay. It's not that easy. Is it?

"You don't need to tell me right this second," Blake says. "But don't string me along."

I swallow and manage to nod. "That's fair."

Step by step, I inch backward toward the window and sit on the sill. Blake and I stare at each other for a minute, or maybe five, until I'm too overwhelmed to stay.

"I should go," I finally whisper.

"Good night, Calvin," he replies.

With that, I tuck and roll out the window, flopping into the plants below.

As I race back to my house, I wonder how I am going to climb into my window again and what in the world I'm supposed to do now.

KENNEDY

Nobody you know saw, Calvin.
Except Jonah. I checked.

I was wrong.

I was mad.

I'm sorry.

Seen.

CHAPTER 40

One "Psst Sarah, let me in" and a sleepless night later, the summer solo is almost here.

I sit in my newly-ordered adult robe that Ms. Clarkson has kindly pinned for me so that it's not two feet too long. This is probably more because she doesn't want me to set Father Paul on fire again, but I appreciate the gesture.

I crinkle the lyrics in my hands. The sheet is so worn from my hundreds—or at least tens—of practices, that I hope I can still read the words when my big moment arrives. As soon as Father Paul finishes the homily, he'll nod to me and my time in the spotlight will begin.

Mom, Dad, and Sarah are in the front row. Mom told Sarah that if she wanted to pull out her phone and secretly film the solo, Mom would pretend she didn't see. I guess this means they're kind of speaking now.

Maia sits by my side. Her family is somewhere in the crowd, and if Sarah's wandering goo-goo eyes are any indication, Anthony and his are out there too. Plus, of course, Mom's friends from Bible Study and all the other congregants I don't know. Quite a turnout for my first foray as Lead Performer.

"Finally," Father Paul says from the pulpit, "I wanted to give a special message to our young followers today."

My neck cranes up, because for some reason, it feels like whatever he says next is going to be about me.

"It has come to my attention"—he clears his throat—"that some of our youths have been sharing things on social media that might not make Jesus especially proud."

Oh my gosh. My face is burning. My head whips toward Maia, who's staring right at me. *It's okay*, she seems to say, but we both know it's not.

"And I know sometimes it feels like the things that people share among friends are safe and harmless, but I have to say something. Jesus sees your Instagram. God reads your tweets. The Holy Spirit is on TikTok. It's important to remember that the things you do now will stay with your soul forever and won't die along with the fifteen seconds of fame a Like may earn."

I can't. How did he even find out? Does Father Paul follow Kennedy on Instagram? Or does he have spies who monitor social media on his behalf and report back to him? I look up toward the sculpted Jesus, His arms spread out. *Was it you?*

I grab Maia's hand because friends hold hands all the time, and wow, do I need a friend. She squeezes.

"Calvin?" Father Paul says, and I can't believe he's specifically calling me out about a post I never even consented to. Everyone is looking at me, and of course I zoned out for like the one second when he was telling everyone what I did. When I don't move, he gestures toward the podium: "Don't you have something to share with everyone now?"

Oh, great. I don't even know why, but I release Maia's hand, rise to my feet, and make my way to the podium. My heart is thumping the whole time. I can't make eye contact with my parents as I walk past. I'm sure they're devastated. This is ridiculous and not fair. So I kissed Blake. And then Jonah. And I like them both. That's not anyone's business. How dare Father Paul think he can call me out in front of everyone like this?

I take the three steps up to the pulpit, flicking my finger around in the sign of the cross on my way. My knuckles clench around the podium.

I scan the crowd, all waiting for me to pour my heart out and beg the Lord for forgiveness. But why should I?

I take a breath, ready to fill the room with excuses, and—

The music begins to play.

I turn toward Ms. Clarkson, who is swaying to the opening chords of "Be Not Afraid."

Oh.

So, this is my solo?

I uncrumple the paper that is still somehow in my hands. I study the words, *You shall cross the barren desert, but you will not die of thirst.* Funny, because somehow my mouth is beyond parched, and I cannot make my lips move to sing this silly song, and the next thing I know, I've leaned into the microphone. "Can I say something for a second?"

Ms. Clarkson looks to Father Paul, lurking somewhere behind me, and the music abruptly stops.

Kennedy promised that nobody I know saw her

post, and I have to believe her. Maybe Father Paul wasn't even talking about me, but if I'm going to really feel "Be Not Afraid" the way Jonah felt the words at his bar mitzvah yesterday, I need to live it.

I can't look at my parents. My heart is racing, but I know I'm ready.

"I think you make a good point, Father Paul, about Instagram and stuff, but here's the thing. Sometimes things happen that maybe you think aren't good as the priest or the adult or whatever, but maybe if you're the person it's happening to, it's not so bad, and maybe it's even great. And sometimes you don't have control over what gets posted either. I should add that because I had no idea."

I'm rambling, just like in the play but I can't stop. All I'm missing is a silver slipper, a couple dozen "forsooth"s, and Jonah to catch me when I fall.

"So yeah, I kissed a boy, and it was all kinds of sweet and confusing, and it tasted like lip balm. I kissed two boys, actually. The second tasted like pasta. Nobody's posted that one yet, but posted or not, there is nothing wrong with me, and Jesus actually texted me yesterday to say He saw it and He Liked it. Okay, that's weird—He didn't say that. But He did see the kisses, and I am still here, and I'm

sorry if it upset you, but I'm sorrier that I upset—"
I stop for a moment because maybe I shouldn't share
their names—"whoever it was I kissed. Which is
nobody's business anyway."

I finally look toward my parents. Dad is actually standing up in the front row. Sarah sits between
them with her phone capturing everything, which
makes me laugh for a second because Mom totally
asked her to do that.

"Anyway," I conclude, "the song is called 'Be
Not Afraid,' and I'm pretty sure I shouldn't sing it
now anyway because I am nothing but afraid and
I'm probably about to be thrown out of this church,
so I will leave you in the very capable hands of my
very good friend, Maia Ruiz, singing whatever she
wants, and I promise you, she has the voice of an
angel."

I nod in Maia's direction, and she stands. A few
shocked people chuckle.

My whole inside is fluttering and shaking. *Don't
fall off the stage. Don't fall off the stage.* I step away from
the podium and start the long walk down the aisle
toward the exit, waiting for anybody to stop me.
Nobody does, although a lot of heads turn when I
walk past. I can hear my parents scrambling to gather

their belongings and follow me out. This might be my last time in this church.

As I reach the doors, I hear Maia's voice on the microphone. "I will be singing 'Tonight' from *West Side Story*." I chuckle because Father Paul is going to kill us all.

Sarah is the first to reach me. I'm sitting in the grass near the spot where the church sets up the manger each Christmas. She kneels by my side and throws her arm around me.

"Cal, most epic confession ever." She's laughing and crying at the same time.

"You'd better not post it," I warn with a sniffly smile.

"Oh, of course not. Not after that homily."

"Are they gonna kill me?" I ask, afraid to look at my parents, who are hanging back on the lawn, letting us sinners have a moment before they swoop in.

"It's gonna be okay," Sarah tells me.

I hear the General whisper, "I wanted to set that guy on fire myself," which is just what you want to hear after you've made a fool of your whole family in front of the entire church. "To make my son feel like that," he continues, and I whip my head around in disbelief. Wait. He's mad at Father Paul? Not me?

Sarah helps me to my feet and stays close behind as I face my parents for the first time since they learned I kissed two boys.

"I'm sorry," I say to both of them. "I know this is a shock, and a disappointment, and—"

"Calvin," Dad cuts me off. "You spoke in front of all those people and you didn't fall down!" He throws his arms around me, which sends me completely off balance.

"Dad, were you listening to what I *said*?"

"Always, son," he replies, which is the nicest lie he's ever told me. He places a hand on each of my shoulders and looks me in the eyes. "I've been waiting for you to tell me since the night we went to Sal's. Before then, really."

"Wait," Mom says to Dad. "You knew?"

Dad shrugs. "There was a leg sticking out of his laundry." He saw that, and he didn't say anything? Was this God's Plan?

"And you're okay with it?" Mom uses the voice of someone who is not quite okay with it. I wait for their marriage to fall apart, but they just stand there processing everything.

"He's our son."

Mom nods, looking kind of dazed. There are tears in her eyes. I wonder if she wants to take me back to confession, but I've kind of already done that today.

"Maia's aunt is gay," I say.

"Mrs. Ruiz's sister?" Mom says with surprise.

"Yep."

"And Mrs. Ruiz knows? She's . . ."

"Perfectly fine with it," I affirm.

Mom takes in this tidbit about one of her dearest friends. The concern on her face turns to relief, and she seems to relax a bit. She takes my father's hand. Maybe it helps to not feel so alone. It's helped me all summer with Maia, Jonah, and Blake. After a moment, Mom says, "Let's go get something to eat. It's been a long morning."

Dad adds, "And maybe some ice cream after?"

"Let's see how we're feeling," Mom says with a cautious nod.

None of this makes sense from the woman who raced Sarah and me to church a couple weeks ago or the man whose three Rs have been set ablaze.

I don't fully trust that we're all good, but as I collapse into my parents' arms in a relieved heap of emotions and Sarah presses in behind me, at least I'm sure that we're okay.

I need to make sure everyone else is too. I look up to my mom, then my dad, and flash my last-day-of-school-photo grin.

"Can I invite a friend?"

I'm as stunned as my parents when they say, "Okay."

I take out my phone and try my best to ignore Sarah as she leans in and swoons in my ear, "But you have to tell me: Jonah or Blake?"

CHAPTER 41

Maia slides into the booth by my side, just in time for ice cream. "Got here as soon as we could," she tells me. "Had to finish my big summer solo."

"How'd it go?" I ask, eager to hear how her turn in the spotlight went and disappointed that I missed it.

"She did a beautiful job," her dad says, taking a seat in the booth right behind us. Her mother, grandmother, and brothers pile in around her dad. I'm so happy they could all finally see what a star she is.

"And next time, maybe she'll sing a church song," Mrs. Ruiz says, throwing Maia a stern look that makes it clear this is not a request.

"Sorry, Mami," Maia says sheepishly before turning to me and sneaking an eye roll. She leans in to whisper, "She's secretly so proud. In the car, she even said maybe I could join my cousin's church choir in Roxbury when the school year starts. We'd take the train to the city every weekend. I think they were getting fed up with Father Paul anyway, and today's sermon did not help. Plus, maybe I'll be a little more . . . seen. I'm not guaranteed a solo or anything, but at least I'll have a fair shot."

"That's amazing," I tell her, and it really is, though I'm going to miss spending the time with her.

"And how're things with you?" She glances at my parents.

Honestly, I have no idea. I texted Jonah and Blake in the car on the way here. I hope you won't be mad, but I told everyone everything.

Jonah replied in seconds: You'll have to be more specific.

I mean everyone: my parents, my sister, the church. Everything.

OMG. Jonah was practically speechless.

And? prompted Blake.

Talk more soon, I replied. I promise.

I know this was only the first step to making things right with him—with both of them—and to figuring out what happens next. But it's a step that didn't pitch me off the stage. That's a decent start.

The door to Cone-y Island swings open, and I swear the temperature drops a few degrees as Kennedy and her dad step inside. She sees Maia and me almost immediately and freezes in the doorway.

She looks up to her dad, practically begging him to turn around. Unfortunately for all of us, her father edges past her and finds a booth somewhere behind ours. Her green eyes scan the floor as she trudges past.

Part of me feels a pang of regret, but another part of me knows that we can't just go back to the way things used to be. Kennedy used me, lied to me, and posted something that wasn't hers to share. Now she comes here and acts like I'm the monster?

"'Scuse me," I say to Maia, tipping my head toward the aisle. She rises to her feet and I slide out of the booth behind her. "I've got to talk to Kennedy," I explain to everyone.

Maia asks with her eyes if I'm sure this is what I want.

Nope, my eyes respond, but I stroll over to Kennedy's table anyway.

Kennedy's dad says, "Hey, Calvin. Fancy meeting you here." His smile is warm, and it makes me sad that he thinks that everything is still okay.

"Good afternoon, Mr. Carmichael," I say with an extra dash of formality to let him know it's not.

Kennedy looks like she's seen a ghost as her eyes connect with mine.

"I'm sorry," she whimpers, and I kind of believe her. "I shouldn't have posted it. I'm awful. I'm a mess."

"I'm sorry you fell," I say, and I actually mean it.

"What can I say? I learn from the best." She laughs, but it's not mean. And for once, she admitted I'm the best.

In that moment, my anger toward Kennedy fades away. When I fell off the stage, Maia tried to catch me, Jonah actually did, and Blake tried to make it all go away. But when Kennedy fell? Her friends at NYYAPA posted it. They memed her. They Kennedied her. I hate this *her* vs. *us* that we have going on here. She was my friend.

Maybe she can be again. One day.

I take a deep breath. "Nobody wants to see you succeed on Broadway more than I do, Kennedy." Relief creeps across her face. "And I know you'll make it one day. But here's some advice."

Kennedy cringes.

"Falling off the stage is easy. Getting up again, that's the hard part. And it helps to have friends. So, if you ever want to talk, let me know. You can find me in the spotlight."

I grab a napkin and one of the crayons that Cone-y Island keeps out for kids. I sign my name and slide the blue autograph in her direction. "And you may want to hold on to this." I spin around feeling like the biggest rock star in all the land. The cape that I know she's picturing flutters behind me.

My phone buzzes in my pocket. Could be Jonah. Could be Blake. Up ahead, my parents, Sarah, Maia, and Maia's family all crane their necks to watch me, an audience on the edge of their seats, wondering what is going to happen next.

Breathe, Calvin. Breathe.

If this summer was dramatic, I can't even imagine what eighth grade will be like. For now, it almost doesn't matter. I survived. With my family, my friends, other patrons, and the staff of Cone-y Island looking on, there is only one thing left to do. I take the bow I never got to take all those months ago when I fell off the stage.

Maia claps loudly.

Sarah lets out a "Yeah, Calvin!" So I take another.

Hesitantly, my parents begin to clap, then Maia's. The other patrons must feel awkward doing nothing, so they join in, one by one. Soon the whole restaurant is cheering for me—the fallen star who's made so many mistakes and gone off script so many times but, for now, has inexplicably brought an audience to its feet.

Forsooth.

Author's Note

What *does* Forsooth even mean?

Calvin redefines the word throughout the book. As I was writing, I found myself repeatedly looking it up to remind myself of its actual definition. According to the dictionary, it's an old-timey sort of exclamation that essentially means "indeed." Truly. Verily. Something you might hear in a knockoff version of *Cinderella*. But to Calvin, it's a reminder of the show he ruined. An insult his classmates use to taunt him. A symbol of his parents' embarrassment. An obstacle he feels he needs to overcome.

I see a parallel between Calvin's relationship with the word *forsooth* and my own Queer identity. I grew up in a conservative Catholic household and did not know what being gay even meant until after I had already experienced crushes I could not explain. Once I learned, it seemed like being gay was fine for others but not a possibility for me. Before understanding and accepting myself, before coming out, I battled thoughts of shame and fear. I heard the words associated with LGBTQIA+ folks used as slurs, sometimes loudly. I worried that I was letting the people I loved down. As a result, I denied who I was for many years.

Thankfully (spoiler alert), by the end of the book, Calvin is able to reclaim the word. *Forsooth* is what makes him stand out in a crowd. It is a celebration of who he has become. The relief, joy, and Pride that Calvin feels as he takes his final bow mirror my own feelings once I came out, accepted myself, even began to love myself.

In truth, Calvin's story is not mine. Everyone's coming out is different. Some journeys are easier than others. Take your time. Do what feels right, safest, best, for you. My hope is that the more stories like Calvin's there are on the shelves, the easier coming out will be, the safer and more welcoming the world will feel. There is room on the stage for all of us. Please know that you are loved. You deserve happiness. You belong. Verily. Truly. Indeed.

Questions for Discussion

1. What do Calvin's most embarrassing moments tell you about Calvin as a person? What hidden strengths do these seemingly disastrous incidents reveal about him?

2. Why is Calvin so upset about Kennedy moving away? Why is Jonah less upset?

3. How does Calvin's movie—both his writing of the screenplay and the attempts to film it—reflect the drama that's going on in his real life?

4. Calvin's mom and dad each seem a certain way on the surface but gradually reveal more about themselves through their actions. How does each parent's behavior compare to Calvin's beliefs about them?

5. Blake tells Calvin, "I've got stuff too, and sometimes I'm not sure you care." What is Blake's stuff? How do you think Calvin can be a better friend to him?

6. Why is Maia frustrated by her experience in church choir? How does Calvin make amends for letting her down?

7. Calvin isn't sure how to approach the subject of race with Jonah, and he gradually realizes he hasn't given it as much thought as he should. What do you think Calvin still has to learn and work on if he's going to be someone Jonah can depend on?

8. Describe Calvin's relationship with Sarah. How does Sarah support Calvin throughout the story?

9. Toward the end of the story, Jonah acknowledges that Calvin isn't perfect and has made a lot of mistakes. Why does Jonah love Calvin anyway?

10. Calvin longs to be a star. What do you think has been holding him back from shining as brightly as he wants to? What helps him gain confidence?

11. What plot lines are resolved at the end of the story? What loose ends are left for Calvin to sort out in the future? What do you think he will do?

12. Calvin is able to calm his anxiety by repeating Blake's mantra of "Breathe" and, later, "Be not afraid." Why do you think he finds these words so steadying?

Acknowledgments

I began writing *Forsooth* at the suggestion of my agent, Emily Keyes. Emily, thank you for believing in Calvin's and my respective journeys. I would not have been brave enough to write this story without your constant support.

Thank you to my beta readers—Sandy, Shoshana, Paige, Courtney, and my writing group—Ben, Rob, Amanda, Sarah, Jen, and Andrew. Your feedback and encouragement truly enriched my earliest drafts. Thank you so much to sensitivity readers Lota Erinne and Larissa Melo Pienkowski for your thoughtful advice.

To blurb writers Adam Sass, Chad Lucas, Emily Barth Isler, and Jason June, I admire your work so much. It's truly an honor and a dream come true to hear you say such kind things about mine. Thank you for your early reads and generous comments.

This book would not be what it is today without my fabulous editor, Amy Fitzgerald. Amy, I could feel your empathy and passion for Calvin's story through your notes, and they left a lasting mark on this book. Thank you for helping me find each character's truth, allowing me to keep some of my more ridiculous lines, and leading Calvin on a kinder journey of self-acceptance. Thank you also to the entire team at Lerner/Carolrhoda, including cover illustrator Marina Pérez Luque, book designer Viet Chu, and production editor Erica Johnson.

Of course, Calvin's story began long before I started writing my first draft. When I was in eighth grade, I auditioned for the title role in my middle school's production of *Oliver*. The music director told me I did a lovely job with my audition song, but asked if I could sing it again and try to sound a little less shaky next time. I assured her I could and tried my best. She proceeded to cast me as a background pickpocket. This was the beginning of the end of my theatrical career. Thank you to my big dreams of superstardom, dashed by stage fright and anxiety, for creating Calvin.

Truthfully, I will never forget my brief few

years on the stage. To my theater crew growing up: Debbie, Alexis, Katie, Jay, Ashley, Casey, Steve, and so many more, thank you for sharing your spotlight with me.

To my parents, who attended every performance, photographed every scene, framed posters signed by every cast, thank you for allowing me to grow on the stage, and thank you for growing with me.

Over the years, my siblings have been my best friends and biggest advocates. Megan, Michael, Robert, and Brian, this story is fictional, but there is so much of you in Calvin's friends and family. Sarah's protectiveness. Blake's calm advice. Maia's humor. Jonah's dedication. Thank you for accepting me from day one.

Natalie, Keira, Norah, Caleigh, and Andrew, it is such a joy to be your uncle. I am so impressed at how cool, talented, funny, and kind you are. I could never. Keep reaching for your dreams. I can't wait to see what you all accomplish next. To my brand-new niece, Ella: hello! I already love you.

To the family I found along the way: Dawn, Marie, and Courtney, what else can I say? <3 Thank you for everything.

Rudy, you are the best boy.

Scott, this book would not exist without your love and advice. There is so much of you in these pages. So much of us. The way you can read ten variations on the same sentence with patience is true love. Thank you for making me laugh like no one else, for holding me through the tears, for loving me when I felt unworthy of love. You are the greatest gift. I am so lucky to call you my husband.

A special shout-out to my therapist, Tim, who has helped me to process all of the above. Taking care of my mental health has been so essential to my journey of self-love, and I am grateful to have found somebody who can help me make sense of it all.

Finally, to my readers, especially my LGBTQIA+ readers, I bow to you and thank you, thank you, thank you.

About the Author

Jimmy Matejek-Morris is a former theater kid and the author of the middle-grade novel *My Ex-Imaginary Friend*. He lives in Massachusetts with his husband, Scott, and a very well-dressed poodle-Pomeranian named Rudy. When he is not writing books and screenplays for young people, you can find Jimmy peeking through the blinds in hopes of spotting baby bunnies or exclaiming "FREE SEED!" so the hungry birds know he has remembered to fill the feeder.